SUNSETS & SECOND CHANCES

RACHEL HANNA

CHAPTER 1

*J*ulie looked back and forth between Dixie and William, like some sort of slow motion tennis game. She didn't know what to say, and Dixie looked particularly dumbfounded and speechless, which was not something she was known for at all.

"William?" Dixie repeated, as she stared at her son.

William was not particularly engaging, his face impassable. It was like they had all invaded his space instead of the fact that he'd shown up at her door on Christmas Day.

"It's me."

"Why don't I leave you two alone?" Julie offered. Dixie grabbed her arm, pulling her gently back to the doorway.

"No. Please stay."

Surprised, Julie stayed put and tried to be like a part of the background. She didn't want to interrupt their reunion after a decade apart. Although, reunions were normally happy, and this one didn't seem to be all that joyous.

"I'm glad to see you, son. How did you find me?"

"It's a small town, Mother. I asked around, and here you are." His voice was so monotone that he sounded like a really annoyed robot.

"Why are you here?" she asked, softly.

"I think you know why."

"Oh," she said, clearing her throat and seeming uncomfortable. "Can I give you a hug?"

He paused for a long moment and then nodded almost imperceptibly. Slowly, Dixie stepped forward and put her arms around his waist, laying her head against his chest. It took a few seconds for William to return her embrace, putting his arms around her loosely. Julie felt awful for Dixie in that moment. Her son was there, but not happily. It was almost worse than not having him there at all.

Julie was confused on his answer as to why he was there. Not wanting to intrude in the moment, she wasn't about to ask.

"Would you like to come in and join us? We're just about to eat," Julie said. He shook his head.

"No, thanks. I'm going to head back to my hotel

room. I just wanted you to know that I'm here in town. We'll speak later."

"William, I'd love if you'd stay and meet my friends. I haven't spent Christmas Day with you in so long."

The look on Dixie's face as she practically begged her only living son to stay for dinner made Julie both sad and angry. This wasn't how anyone should treat Dixie.

"Everything okay over here?" Dawson asked as he walked up next to Julie. Having him standing beside her made her feel safe in an inexplicable way.

"Dawson?" William said, obviously surprised to see him there.

"Will. Good to see you." Julie could feel the tension in the air. Dawson definitely seemed on edge.

"You live here?"

"No. This is Julie's house. I still live at the inn."

"Oh. Maybe we can catch up sometime soon."

Dawson smiled, but it was really more of a smirk. "Sure. After you spend some time with your mother, of course. I think she's earned it."

William glared at Dawson, and Julie worried a fist fight might break out. That's all she needed on Christmas Day, a big brawl in her newly decorated living room.

"We honestly have too much food. Why don't you stay a bit and at least have something to eat?" Julie asked, not really wanting this man in her house, but feeling the need to do it for Dixie.

William took in a deep breath and slowly blew it out. "Okay," he said, not making eye contact with anyone as he walked in the door.

Everyone else had been talking and not really noticing the unbelievably awkward situation happening at the front door. Dixie walked in front of her son, pointing at people and introducing them. William did the requisite "nice to meet you" tour and then walked to the dining room to take a seat.

Julie had set up an extra long folding table too, just in case they had anyone else drop by. Now, she was thankful she did.

"I just want to thank everyone for being here today," Julie said, as she stood up with her glass of sweet tea. "I can't think of a better way to spend Christmas than with all of the people who have helped me through a very challenging time in my life. I'm so grateful for all of you."

Everyone clinked their glasses and then started digging into the food. Dawson sat on her left, her sister on her right. She had a full view of Dixie and her son sitting at the folding table, Dixie's original seat empty at the main table.

"This is awkward," Dawson whispered in her ear.

"Tell me about it. But, I felt like I had to invite him in for Dixie's sake." She plopped a scoop of mashed potatoes on her plate and passed them to her sister.

"That guy's strange," Janine said.

"He didn't used to be. He was a cool guy. But, the way he's treated Dixie is wrong, and I plan to tell him that."

"Dawson, maybe you shouldn't interfere," Julie said softly.

He looked at her. "She's like a mother to me. I have to say something."

Julie nodded, not wanting to upset him on Christmas. She was new to this whole dynamic, so she trusted that Dawson knew best.

"Well, if one of my kids acted like that, I'd cut them off for good," SuAnn said, having obviously been updated on the history by Janine.

"Mom, you would not. We've had our fair share of tiffs over the years, and you're currently sitting at my table," Julie said, rolling her eyes.

"Apology accepted," SuAnn said, blowing a fake kiss at her daughter.

"Very funny."

"So, what's everyone doing after we eat?" Janine asked.

"Doing? I'm planning on a nice long nap and a big glass of wine, probably not in that order," Julie said.

"I sure hope you're not drinking too much," SuAnn chided.

"Oh, Mother," Julie said, rolling her eyes again. She did that a lot when SuAnn was around, although it would've gotten her a slap across the face if she'd done it as a kid. SuAnn hated eye rolling, which was a big reason Julie did it. Childish, but oh so effective.

"Well, Buddy and I are going to drive and see the Christmas lights in Charleston and then stay a night there before driving home."

"I thought you were staying here tonight?" Julie said.

SuAnn looked at Buddy and smiled. "Well, dear, I don't want to be crude, but we need a little alone time, if you get my drift."

"I just threw up a little in my mouth," Janine said, putting her hand to her lips.

"Oh nonsense! Sex between a married couple is important. Without it, you're really just roommates," SuAnn said, slapping Buddy's leg. He chuckled and went back to his plate of food. Julie swore the man never spoke.

"Mother! Honestly! Let's not talk about sex at the Christmas dinner table."

"Fine," SuAnn said, taking a bite of her food.

Julie leaned over to Dawson. "Sorry about my mother," she whispered. "She has no filter, and it's only getting worse."

Dawson chuckled. "I'm actually enjoying it. Normally, it's just me and Lucy having Christmas dinner together. This year, she's with her family now that they live local again."

"Well, I'm glad this year is different."

He smiled. "Me too."

"I wonder how their conversation is going," Julie said, looking over at Dixie and William. They were sitting across from each other, neither making eye contact. Dixie was picking at her food, probably too nervous to eat.

"Doesn't look like much conversation is happening," Dawson said, as he held a fork full of green beans up to his mouth.

"I wish I knew how to help her."

"He seems like kind of a jerk," Janine butted in.

Dawson nodded. "He is now. He didn't used to be. We were pretty tight back in the day."

"Back in the day?" Julie said, laughing.

"Don't the kids still say that?"

"I don't think so," Janine said with a chuckle.

"Well, I hope Dixie gets what she needs out of this visit," Julie said, worried about her friend.

"Me too. But, I think there's more to this story. I don't know why he suddenly showed up," Dawson said.

"I'm not sure, but I plan to find out."

~

Christmas had been a whirlwind, so Julie was more than happy to get back to work at the bookstore. The rush of customers hadn't stopped all the way up to Christmas Eve, and now they were back for the after Christmas sales.

Dixie had decided before the holidays that they would mark down a bunch of books and have a sidewalk sale the day after Christmas. Customers were clamoring for the good deals, and Julie was having a hard time keeping up with everything by herself. She was thrilled to see Dixie show up just before lunchtime to help her.

"Sorry, I'm late. William and I had breakfast this morning." She didn't look happy about it.

"How'd it go?" Julie asked as she bagged up the last customer's books. Thankfully, it seemed everyone in town was taking a lunch break at the same time. She needed a breather.

"Not well." Dixie sighed and sat down in one of the bistro chairs. She looked tired.

"I'm so sorry. Is there anything I can do?"

She smiled sadly. "Short of being the world's best therapist, I'm not sure anyone can help. He's just still so angry at me."

"About Johnny?"

"Yeah, that's most of it. But, he seems to have added new grievances over the years, like he's been stewing on all the ways I failed him as a mother. I just don't know what to do."

"I don't understand something. Why did he come back if he's mad at you?"

Dixie took in a deep breath and blew it out. "There's something I haven't told you, dear."

"What?"

"I've been having some medical problems. That was one reason I wanted to hire you."

"Medical problems? But, you seem as spry as anyone I know, Dixie. Is it something they can fix?"

"Not really. I have Parkinson's disease."

Julie felt like the wind had been knocked out of her. She didn't know much about the disease, but she knew it was progressive. The last person who deserved an awful disease was Dixie. She was a saint of a woman and seemed immortal.

"But, I haven't seen you shaking or anything."

Dixie smiled. "The miracle of modern medicine. The tremors are under control. But the medication makes me very tired. And there's something else."

"What?"

"My memory has been a little spotty in recent months. My neurologist was concerned enough to ask me to reach out to my family for extra support. So, I sent a letter to William just before you moved to town. Honestly, had I known the daughter I always wanted was going to appear in my life, I might not have contacted my son."

Julie thought about whether Dixie had seemed forgetful lately. There was one time where a huge book order came in, and Dixie didn't remember ordering it. But the holiday rush could make anyone stressed out, so Julie had chalked it up to that.

"Oh, Dixie, I'm so sorry. How can I help?"

"Now, I don't want to be pitied. That's why I haven't told anyone. I'm a proud old bird, you know."

Julie laughed. "That you are. But, why did William come if he's still so angry?"

"I 'spose he wants to make sure he gets my possessions once I kick the bucket. I don't really know."

"I hope that's not why he came."

"Me too. Well, enough about sad stuff. How's it going with Dawson?"

Julie grinned like a schoolgirl. "He's pretty great."

"Yes, he is. Are y'all officially an item then?"

"Not really. I mean, we've gone on a few informal dates, but we're taking it slow. After my divorce, I don't know if I'm ready to jump back into a relationship again."

"Don't let that scoundrel of an ex husband ruin your chance at real happiness. Life is short."

"I know. I guess we'll see how things go. I'm going to go start cleaning up the store a bit. Why don't you relax and get some sunshine?" Julie stood and started walking toward the door.

"Don't treat me like I'm old and sick," Dixie chided. "I'm still fit as a fiddle!"

"I know, I know..." Julie said, laughing as she disappeared into the store.

"Parkinson's?" Janine said, her mouth hanging open. "But, she seems so healthy and vibrant, even for her age."

"I know. But, I've done some research about the disease since she told me, and I didn't realize all of the other symptoms that came with it."

"Like what?"

"Well, like freezing."

"Freezing? Like cold?"

"No. People will often just freeze up, like when they're walking or tying their shoes. And then there are non-motor symptoms like swallowing problems, dizziness, insomnia, loss of smell, urinary issues..."

"Please stop. It's making me sad."

"People with Parkinson's usually live long lives, but I do think we need to help her find resources. Dixie is a proud woman, but there are some great rehab opportunities for people with the disease. I'm going to look into them and see what I can find."

"I'll help however I can. Gentle yoga would be great for her balance too. I'll suggest it next time I see her."

"Thanks, sis. So, I assume Mom and Buddy are heading toward the mountains by now?"

"Yes, thank goodness. I love her, but I can only take her in small doses."

Julie giggled. "I quite enjoyed talking about sex over the Christmas ham."

Janine's eyes widened. "I know, right? What is wrong with her sometimes?"

"Hello, ladies," Dawson said as he walked into the house. Julie was used to him coming and going like he lived there. He was always fixing this or that, and she enjoyed the familiarity they'd developed.

"Hey," Julie said, motioning for Janine to leave. Janine slipped out the front door, probably to take one of her long walks.

"How was work?"

"Good. Listen, I had a talk with Dixie today."

"And?"

"Dawson, she has Parkinson's disease," Julie blurted out. She had never been great at delivering difficult news.

"What? When did she find this out?"

"A few months ago. She hasn't told anyone. Well, except for William. That's apparently why he came back."

"That makes a lot more sense. Do you think he wants her money?"

"I don't know, but I think we're going to have to watch him carefully. Dixie's already dealing with enough. I don't want this to be a setback for her."

"Me either. You know, I'm so thankful she has

you, Julie. You moving to Seagrove has been a godsend for so many people."

Julie smiled. "Oh, yeah? Like who?"

Dawson shrugged his shoulders, the corner of his mouth rising up to create that adorable dimple he had on one side. "Well, Dixie, for one. And Janine. And…"

"And?" she said, staring up at him.

"And maybe this guy right here." He pointed to himself. "I was getting a little lonely on this island."

"Glad I could help relieve your loneliness," she said softly. The romantic tension between them had been building for months, but they hadn't gotten any further than hand holding and very long hugs. Julie didn't understand it. He seemed interested in her, but not one kiss. She was starting to lose hope.

"Listen, I have a question."

"Okay. Shoot."

"Would you be my date for New Year's Eve? We have a big party here on the island, over on the beach. Some of the mainland people come. There's a DJ, dance floor, food…"

"I'd love to," Julie interjected. Kissing would most definitely be happening on New Year's Eve. If she had to maul the poor man, she would.

There was a part of her that knew she was stepping into dangerous territory. Her brain was in a constant fight back and forth about getting in a new relationship. On the one hand, Dawson was amazing. He was handsome, kind, talented and loyal. But she'd thought many of the same things about Michael at one time. He'd been loyal. Until he wasn't.

Taking a chance on a man again wasn't something she did lightly. It was much easier to be alone and protect her heart. But she did get lonely. She wanted that connection with a man again. She wanted strong arms around her when the world seemed to be falling apart. She wanted someone to talk to, to confide her deepest thoughts to. Vulnerability was hard and dangerous. The conflict she felt was exhausting.

What she didn't get was why Dawson was going so slowly. Was he unsure of their budding relationship? Was he only interested in her as a friend? Had he spoken too soon about wanting to start something with her?

"Really? Great. I'm excited. It's a fun party, and you'll get to meet more people around here."

Maybe he was just taking her to meet people. Maybe he wasn't planning on kissing her at the stroke of midnight. Why did she care so much? It wasn't like she was back in high school, hoping the cute boy in her math class was going to ask her out. He never did.

"Can't wait."

"I'll pick you up at eight. Sound good?"

"Sounds great!"

"Okay. I'd better run. I agreed to have an early dinner with William on the mainland."

"Really?"

"Yes. And I have a lot of questions for him."

Julie smiled. "Don't get put in jail. I need a date for this party."

Dawson chuckled. "I'll try. No promises, though."

CHAPTER 2

*D*awson sat at the table near the water's edge and stared out over the vast ocean. He loved this place, his home. It was in his blood. He couldn't imagine ever living anywhere else. And now that he knew Julie, he couldn't imagine her living anywhere else either. She didn't seem like a city woman anymore. At first, she'd definitely seemed like a fish out of water, and he liked to think he had something to do with her transformation.

She was special. It made him nervous to think about just how special she was to him. No one had made him feel this way since Tania, his late wife. But, lately, he'd been having such vivid dreams of her, looking at him in a way that made him feel guilty for finally thinking about moving on. Had his son, Gavin, survived his birth, he'd be in high school now. It made him sad to think about it, but he couldn't avoid it sometimes. The memories just came like unwelcome guests, setting up house in his brain and making him feel things he'd rather not.

Imagining what it would be like to play football with him in the yard. Teaching him how to tie a tie for his first homecoming dance. Giving him unwanted, cheesy Dad advice about girls. He'd missed out on so much.

After losing his child, he'd never had the desire to have more kids. Something in him just died that day. Maybe it was the part that was excited about becoming a father. All he knew was that the only child he'd ever have was Gavin, even if he was his guardian angel now.

"Hey." William's voice broke his concentration. He stood beside the table, towering over Dawson. Although, if Dawson stood up, he'd tower over William.

"Hey. Sit, please."

William sat down and looked at the water, probably wanting to avoid Dawson's intense gaze. Finally, he looked at him.

"It's been a long time," William finally said, probably getting tired of the glare Dawson was giving him.

"You know I love Dixie like she's my own mother, right?"

"That's how I remember it, yes," William said, dryly.

17

"I want to know why you've done this to her."

"Done what to her, Dawson?" he asked, his jaw tightening.

"Seriously? You abandoned your mother, man!"

"Hi... Um, can I get you guys something to drink?" the young, female server asked, nervous from obviously walking into a hornet's nest.

"Sweet tea, please," Dawson said, being sure to smile at her. No need to be rude to the server when he only really wanted to strangle William.

"Water with lemon," William said, not making eye contact with her.

"I'm sorry he's being rude," Dawson said to the server. "Constipation," he whispered. She let out a laugh and quickly ran away.

"Constipation? Really? Very mature," William said, rolling his eyes.

"Just about as mature as you've been acting for the last ten years."

"Look, Dawson, I don't owe you an explanation. I don't even know why I came here," he said, standing up.

"Sit down," Dawson said, rising up slightly.

William's lips pursed as he sucked in a sharp breath and sat back down. Even as kids, he never crossed Dawson. Though he was a nice guy all the way to his core, he was big and tall and had a presence about him.

"I don't know what you want me to say."

"I want to know why you left your mother here alone for all these years."

William sighed. "I blamed her for Daddy's death."

"That's insane, man. Surely you know that."

"She didn't make him have chemo or any kind of treatment. She just watched him waste away, and there was nothing I could do. She had the power."

"Will, that's not even true. You know Johnny was one of the most stubborn people I've ever known. He told Dixie that he didn't want to spend his last months with poison in his veins."

"That's what she says."

"And I know your Dad must have told you the same thing."

William grumbled. "Maybe she talked him into not doing it. I mean, my Daddy had a fat insurance policy. Maybe…"

Dawson slammed his hand on the table, shaking the silverware, just as the poor server walked up to the table with their drinks. She looked at him for a moment before setting them on the table.

"Thanks," he said, smiling up at her and hoping he hadn't scared her. She slowly walked away, looking back once more before disappearing into the building.

"Jeez, I see you're still intense, Dawson. You almost scared that girl to death." He took a long sip of his water as he eyed his old friend.

Dawson sucked in a sharp breath and let it out.

"I'm not intense. That part of me matured long ago. But, I am protective of Dixie."

William laughed, not in a jovial way, but more of an ironic one. "She's my mother. Shouldn't I be the protective one?"

"You'd think so," Dawson said. "But, you let her down a long time ago."

"Well, sorry I let you down too, old friend." He rolled his eyes and turned to look out over the water.

"You've let your mother down most of all."

"Yeah, well she let me down a decade ago when my father took his last breath. She could've saved him. I know it in my bones, man. He would've listened to her if she had just kept pushing."

"Look, Will, I know losing your Dad was hard. I get it. I lost my wife. My kid. My brother. My parents. My grandma. The difference is I didn't blame anyone. Sometimes, bad things happen. Nobody's fault."

"If I believed that my Daddy really didn't want treatment, then I have to believe he wanted to die. That he didn't care enough about his only son to at least try. And my Dad wasn't a quitter. He wouldn't have done that to me."

"So the only choice is to blame your mother? What would your father think of that?"

"I've got to go. I have an appointment," William suddenly said, standing up and throwing a few bucks on the table, even though all he ordered was water.

"An appointment?"

"Job interview." William started to walk away.

"Wait. You're staying here?"

"Yes. I'm home for good."

JULIE STRAIGHTENED the books on the shelf, little plumes of dust occasionally billowing into the air. Down Yonder was the coziest bookstore she'd ever been in, but also the dustiest. It wasn't like those big, retail bookstores that were always clean and tidy and bright. Instead, it had character, a wandering dog and those little dust bunnies that formed when no one picked up certain books for weeks on end.

"So, when is your next appointment with the doctor?" she asked Dixie, who was hanging new business cards on the bulletin board.

"Thursday," she said in her sing songy way, obviously doing her best to pretend nothing was wrong.

Julie cleared her throat. "Is William going with you?"

Dixie chuckled. "I would highly doubt it. I don't even know why he came back. None of it makes any sense to me."

"Have you talked since Christmas?" Julie asked, walking back to the counter. It had only been a couple of days, but the tension around the situation was so thick, it felt like weeks.

"Here and there, but not much. He's living at a hotel, and I invited him to come home, to his old room. He was adamantly against that. I just don't know what to do or say."

Julie reached over and put her hand on Dixie's. "He came back for a reason. I'm sure he'll come around soon enough. Just give him space and let him come to you, like one of those scared dogs you try to lure into your car. If you come on too strong, they run away. But, if you just ignore them and sit on the curb, they'll come right over to you."

Dixie giggled. "That's a weird comparison, but I see what you mean." She turned and picked up her purse. "I'm awfully tired this afternoon. Do you mind if I go home and put my feet up for the rest of the day?"

"Hey, you're the boss!" Julie said. "And if you need anything, and I do mean anything, please let me know, okay?"

Dixie smiled. "I don't know what I'd do without you, hon."

"Ditto."

After Dixie left, Julie's phone rang. She looked down to see Meg calling from Europe. Meg only called on Sundays, and it was only Wednesday, so Julie was immediately concerned.

"Meg? What's wrong?"

Meg laughed. "Wow, Mom, you might need to take some anxiety medication. Why would you think something's wrong?"

Julie let out the breath she'd been holding and lowered her shoulders from her ears. "You don't usually call during the week, sweetie."

"You don't want to hear from me?"

Julie sat down on the vintage sofa Dixie had put in her Gone With The Wind section of the bookstore. "Of course I want to hear from either one of my girls. I miss you both so much."

Starting over alone had been hard, even with all of her new friends around. She ached to hug her girls, to be their mom all the time again. Funny how she'd often complained when they were kids, about all of the carting them around, paying for everything and their loud parties with friends at her house almost every weekend. And then suddenly, life was quiet. It was oddly unsettling.

"I just need to tell you something."

Butterflies fluttered around Julie's stomach. Was it ever a good thing when a kid said they needed to talk to a parent? Not in her experience.

"Okay. What's up?"

"I'm in love, Mom."

Julie paused and said nothing for a few moments. While Colleen had always been the one dating boys in high school, Meg had been less social. She'd had friends, but no dates, really. She skipped dances and opted to read books in her room instead. She was studious, which was why she'd gotten such an amazing opportunity to study abroad. Of course, Julie had always prayed she'd meet a great guy one day, get married and have a bunch of babies she could spoil. But she was only nineteen and living in a foreign country, which made Julie feel very much out of control.

"You're in love?" Julie said softly.

"Yes. He's amazing, Mom! I met him at a coffee shop near campus, and we just hit it off so well. He teaches art history at the university."

"He's a professor?" Julie didn't have a good feeling about this. Dating someone in a power position wasn't always the best idea, especially for a young woman so far from home and those who loved her.

"Yes, but don't worry. I'm not in any of his classes."

Don't worry? Yeah, right.

"What's his name?"

"Christian."

"How old is he, Meg?"

She was silent for a long moment. "He's thirty-one."

"What?" Julie couldn't contain herself. Her voice, several octaves above its normal tone, pierced through the phone.

"Mom, don't freak out. That's why I waited so long to tell you."

"So long? How long?"

"Two months."

"Meg! I can't believe you waited that long!"

"I knew you'd freak over his age."

Julie tried to get herself together. The last thing she wanted to do was leave her daughter feeling like she couldn't talk to her. As far away as she was, she needed to have a connection to Meg to make sure she was safe.

"Honey, what could you possibly have in common with a man of his age?"

"He gets me, Mom," she said, speaking in a way Julie had never heard her daughter speak. She sounded like a middle school girl talking about her first crush, and it worried Julie that she wasn't thinking clearly. "We like going to museums, eating croissants, dancing. He loves me."

"Meg, I just hope you're being level headed about this. I don't want you to get hurt."

"Christian would never hurt me, Mom."

"I didn't think your Dad…" Julie said, before stopping herself. She hadn't meant to blurt that out. She didn't want to make her daughters jaded about all men just because of what their father had done to her. "I'm sorry. I shouldn't have said that."

"It's okay, Mom. I know it's still fresh."

"I'm glad you called me, Meg."

"Me too. We'll talk more soon, okay?"

"Okay. Meg?"

"Yeah?"

"Be careful, okay? You're so far away, and I feel so helpless." A stray tear fell from her eye.

"I will, Mom. Don't worry about me. I've never been this happy in my life."

"I'm glad, sweetie. I love you."

"Love you too."

Julie ended the call and sighed, leaning her head back against the couch. One more thing to worry about. Did mothers ever have a time when they didn't worry? She wondered what that would be like.

"WHERE ARE WE GOING?" Julie asked as she held Dawson's hand. He'd put a blindfold on her and was leading her down a path of crunchy leaves. After a long day at work and the worrisome call from Meg, just holding his hand made her feel better than she'd care to admit.

"That would ruin the surprise, now wouldn't it?"

"I suppose."

She continued following him until she started hearing the ocean in the distance. The breeze hit her face, and the familiar scent of salty air wafted up her nose. She licked her lips and tasted the saltiness on them.

"The beach?" she asked.

"Not telling you a thing, woman," he said, with a laugh. Finally, they stopped and he touched both of her shoulders. "Sit down."

She slowly crouched down and then landed on her rear end. She reached down and felt what must have been a plush blanket. Dawson reached around her head and untied the blindfold.

Julie looked around. They were on a part of the beach she'd never been to. It was remote, no houses anywhere in view. The sun was starting to set, wisps of pink and orange racing across the sky, glimmers of the last bits of orange sunlight streaking across the water. The beauty of the scene almost made her cry. When she turned to look back at Dawson, she noticed the picnic set out on the blanket in front of her.

"Dawson, you didn't have to do this!"

"You deserve a little down time. I don't think you've had any since you got here."

She smiled. "Thank you. And look at this food!"

"All thanks to Lucy, of course."

Julie looked around and saw chicken salad sandwiches, fruit and a bottle of wine. Simple, yet so thoughtful.

"She also made peach cobbler, but I have it in the insulated warmer thing she sent with me," he said, pointing behind him.

"Is that the technical name for it?"

"I do believe so."

"Seriously, thank you, Dawson. I needed this. Where are we, anyway?"

"This is Hell's Point."

"What kind of name is that?"

Dawson laughed as he poured two glasses of wine. "Legend has it that pirates used to get marooned here in their ships because they didn't see this narrow piece of land jutting out into the sea. We've even had treasure hunters come here over the years, searching for the supposed gold coins they would often leave here after shipwrecks."

Julie took a sip of wine. "Interesting. I could use some treasure right now."

"Me too."

"My daughter called me today."

"Oh yeah? Which one?"

"Meg, the one in France. She had some news."

"What kind of news?"

"I don't really know what to think about it. She has a new boyfriend. Says she's in love. She's nineteen and he's thirty-one."

Dawson's face didn't change. "And you don't like their age difference?"

"What could they really have in common?"

He smiled. "Spoken like a worried mother."

"She's thousands of miles away in a foreign country, and now she's dating a guy old enough to…"

"To what? Be her older brother?"

She laughed. "I guess he couldn't be her father."

"Not unless he had a child when he was twelve, no."

"I am worried, Dawson. What if this guy is a maniac? What if he hurts her? What if…"

"What if he breaks her heart like her father did to her mother?" He took a sip of his wine, crouching behind his glass like he was hiding from her.

"I know that's part of it. How couldn't I worry about that? I don't ever want my daughters to get hurt like that. I thought everything was good in my marriage. I really did. And then it hit me out of the blue like a lightning bolt."

"Julie, I know you love your girls. And I know you want to protect them. But, let me ask you something."

"Okay."

"If one of your friends had told you a year ago that your husband was going to hurt you, would it have changed anything?"

She thought for a moment. "No. I wouldn't have believed them. I thought I knew him."

"Exactly. Nothing you say to Meg is going to change her mind about this guy. And you risk pushing her away if you judge him without even meeting him."

"You're right. How are you always right?" she asked with a smile.

He sighed. "I'm not always right, trust me."

"Oh, you had your dinner with William last night, didn't you?"

"I did."

"And how did it go?"

"Not the best. He's so different than he used to be. Will was a cool guy when we were growing up. He had a great sense of humor, and you could count on him, ya know? But, now he seems like a different person. I lit into him about the way he treated his Mom, but I don't know if it made any difference."

"I'm sorry. Dixie is just so broken up about all of it. She doesn't know what to do. In fact, she left early from work to get some rest. I'm worried about her."

"Do you think she'd let you go to her doctor appointment if you offered?"

"I don't know, but I'm going to ask. Somebody should be there, be her advocate. That's so important."

Dawson smiled at her. "I'm so glad you came into our lives, Julie Pike."

Julie felt redness moving across her cheeks. Dang pale complexion always gave her away. "Thank you."

"No, really. Getting to know you has been one of the great joys of my life so far. As you can imagine, living on this island can get a bit lonely."

She smiled. "I can understand that. This is the quietest place I've ever been."

"After I lost my wife, I honestly thought I'd spend my life alone. I mean, there aren't a lot of single women on the island, and who would want this quiet little life I love so much?"

She wanted to raise her hand, but thought better of it. "It's not a bad life, Dawson."

"I'm what most would refer to as a simple man. Most of the women I've met are much faster paced than I am."

"The world is pretty fast paced."

"True. Look, I guess what I'm trying to say is I know I might move really slow compared to a lot of men, but I want you to know I am interested in building a relationship with you, Julie. I mean, if you're interested."

The redness moved up toward her cheeks again. "I'm definitely interested."

Dawson smiled broadly. "Good. I just didn't want you to take my slow speed for me not being interested. I know it's been years since I lost my wife and baby, but it's still fresh for me sometimes. And these feelings I have for you... well, it's just that it's been a long time..."

Julie reached over and held his hand. "I get it. Even though my husband is a jerk of the highest order, there are parts of me that feel like I'm being unfaithful. It's silly, especially since he did what he did to me, but I never expected to be a divorced woman."

"You're a good person, Julie."

"So are you, Dawson. Now, shall we dig into these sandwiches? Because I'm starving!"

～

JANINE STRETCHED her arms over her head, reaching toward the sky as she closed her eyes and sucked in a deep breath of the salty air. She'd never realized how much she loved the ocean until she'd ended up in Seagrove. This place felt like home, and no place had ever felt that way to her.

After spending most of her life going from place to place, working this job and that, she finally felt stable and at peace. Reconnecting with her sister had been an unexpected blessing, and now that she was about to start her own yoga business, she finally felt like her life was on track.

Mornings were her favorite time to be on the beach. No one else was there but her and the curious seagulls who seemed to be convinced she had snacks. Occasionally, she'd throw out some granola, but they didn't seem particularly interested in it.

It was only a few weeks before her classes opened to the public. She'd be teaching on the stretch of beach behind Dawson's house. So far, ten women had already expressed an interest, and she was excited to teach them. When the feeling of nervousness started to kick in, she pushed it away with breathing techniques as best she could.

She sat down on her mat and crossed her legs. Closing her eyes, she spent a few minutes breathing in the clean ocean air and breathing out her worries and fears. Meditation was something that fueled her and kept her sane, even during the worst of times. It had been her only help in the months after her attack, when no one else knew or could help. Counseling and meditation had saved her, and she was thankful that her sister had stepped in to help her when she was at her rock bottom.

She laid back against her mat, her eyes still closed as she felt the morning sun start to beat down on her body. It was a warm day, even for late December, but not warm enough to swim. She wore her favorite yoga pants and a long sleeve tee, her thick, curly hair pulled into a messy bun atop her head.

One of her favorite games as a kid was looking at the puffy white clouds in the sky and deciding what animal they looked like. Today, the sky was a beautiful, rich blue, and there were no clouds to be seen. She watched overhead as an airplane made its way across the vast blueness and wondered where it was going. It wasn't so long ago that she was in airplanes, traveling all over the world looking for herself. Who knew she'd find herself on a small island off the coast of South Carolina? Life was funny sometimes.

She closed her eyes again, deciding to relax her mind. Just as she was drifting off to sleep, suddenly freezing cold water assaulted her body, causing her to sit straight up in a panic. She wiped her eyes and opened them, barely able to make out the blurry person standing in front of her. It seemed to take minutes, but was probably only a few seconds, when her eyes finally cleared and she saw William standing there.

"Why did you pour water on me?" she asked, angrily, as she glared at him.

He was wearing board shorts and a t-shirt, like it was the middle of summer, and carrying some kind of board. Seagrove wasn't exactly a great place to surf, so she couldn't imagine what he was doing.

William smirked and then rolled his eyes. "I didn't pour water on you, lady. I rode my board in and it must have tossed water on you when I picked it up."

Janine knew it wasn't an accident. He could've ridden his board back onto land in another spot on the vast beach, but he chose right where she was laying? She stood up.

"Isn't a little bit cold to be out in the water, anyway?"

Again, he smirked. "I grew up here. I'm used to it."

"So, you're surfing? I don't see any waves."

"I'm not surfing. I'm stand up paddle boarding."

Janine had heard of that when she was in Bali a few years back. She'd always wanted to learn, especially since it was supposed to strengthen core muscles. She definitely needed that after being out of practice with her yoga for so long. Teaching yoga would help her get back into shape, but she wanted to be at the top of her game.

"Is it hard to learn?" she asked.

He shrugged his shoulders. "Depends on what kind of shape you're in. I mean, pardon me for saying so, but you seem a little..."

"A little what?"

"Weak."

Janine wanted to wring his neck. "Excuse me? You don't know a thing about me."

"I know you eat granola and do yoga, and you seem to 'relax' a lot." He did air quotes around "relax", which made her even angrier.

"That's a stereotypical response. People who do yoga are some of the strongest you'll ever meet! And, as for my 'relaxing', that's called meditation. You might want to try it sometime." She leaned down and started rolling up her mat, as it was obvious her peaceful spot had been intercepted.

"No, thanks. Seems like a big waste of time to me," he said, turning to walk toward the path back to the road.

"Somebody like you needs it," she mumbled. He stopped and turned around.

"What's that supposed to mean?"

She walked closer and eyed him carefully. "As someone who has experienced trauma, I can tell that you have some stuff to work out in that head of yours. If you ever need help with that, you know where to find me every morning." Without saying another word, she walked past him and headed for the road.

CHAPTER 3

*J*ulie sat beside Dixie in the waiting room. Why did doctor's offices always have such old magazines? Half of the celebrities on the front were already broken up. Julie had offered to go to the appointment with a new movement disorder specialist with Dixie, so they had closed the bookstore a few hours early.

"Why can't these doctors ever be on time? If I was late, they'd charge me a fee, but they can be half an hour late and I'm supposed to just sit here," Dixie said. She wasn't herself today. She was angry and bobbing her leg up and down, not from Parkinson's tremors but anxiety. Julie felt for her and wished she could fix the whole situation.

"Ms. Campbell?" the nurse called from the doorway. It occurred to Julie that she'd never asked

Dixie's last name, yet they'd been friends all these months.

Dixie stood and turned to Julie. "You're coming, right?"

Julie nodded, thankful that Dixie wanted her in the room. She needed to understand more about Parkinson's and how it was affecting her friend.

After taking her blood pressure and weight, they put them in a room. Thankfully, the doctor came in quickly. He did a series of neurological tests, having Dixie squeeze his hands, follow his finger with her eyes and walk up and down the hallway. Once he was finished, they followed him to his office and sat down across from his desk.

"Well, doc, what's the verdict?" Dixie asked, trying to play it off in her normal fashion.

"I definitely believe you have the early stages of Parkinson's. However, this is a very slow progressing disease. People don't usually die *of* Parkinson's, they die *with* it. At your age and with your symptoms, I fully expect you to live a long, normal life."

"What about the memory lapses I'm having?"

"I looked over your medication list, and I saw a sleeping pill you're taking?"

"Yes. My primary care doctor gave me that a few months ago when I was having trouble sleeping."

"Parkinson's has many symptoms, one of which

is insomnia or constantly waking up during the night."

"I was having both problems."

"I'd like to try you on a different sleeping medication. The one you're on can have the side effect of memory issues. So, I'd prefer to cross that off the list of culprits before we worry about memory loss or early dementia."

Dixie squirmed in her seat. "Dementia?"

The doctor smiled reassuringly. "I don't think you have dementia right now, but it is a possible effect of the Parkinson's. A substantial percentage of patients do go on to develop dementia at some point. That's why it's important to tell your family what you want now, as far as treatment options, living arrangements and so forth."

Dixie looked shellshocked. Julie reached over and took her hand.

"Are there medications that Dixie can take?"

"Dr. Arnold already has her on medication for her tremors, and it seems to be working well. It can cause fatigue, and maybe a little depression, so I'd like to give you an antidepressant to try, if you're open to that."

"You know, I lost my son and my husband and never took a pill for that. I just can't imagine that I need an antidepressant for this."

Julie smiled and squeezed her hand. "Dixie, if it

will help, maybe you should just try it. Life's too short to be miserable, right?"

Dixie sighed and nodded her head. "Okay. I guess I'll try it."

Dr. Holmes smiled. "Good. And I'd like to start you on our physical therapy program here too. It will help you keep in shape, and that's the best treatment for Parkinson's. We've found that vigorous exercise is the best weapon we have to combat the disease."

"How often will I need to do this? I run a bookstore."

"Probably twice a week to see how you do. Then you'll have some at home exercises to do as well."

"Don't worry, Dixie. I can work as often as you need," Julie said, patting her leg.

Dixie smiled gratefully. "What would I do without you?" Hearing her say that reminded her of what Dawson had said at the beach. It made her feel good to be needed again.

As they drove back to Dixie's house, Julie kept going over the information the doctor had given them. She worried about Dixie's prognosis, but she was also hopeful that the medication changes would help her live a long, productive life.

"You're awfully quiet over there," Julie said.

"Just thinking about everything. So much to take in."

"I know, but don't you worry. I'll be there for you no matter what."

Dixie reached over and patted her leg. "I appreciate you more than you'll ever know. Wait. Isn't today New Year's Eve?"

"Yes, it is," Julie said with a laugh.

"Hard to keep up with these days lately. So, you and Dawson have a date tonight, right?" She grinned like a Cheshire cat.

"We're going to the big party on the island."

"So, a date?"

"I honestly don't know what to call it. I just know he wants to take it slowly, and I'm okay with that."

"Are you?"

"Of course I am! I just got out of a very long marriage. I don't want to jump into anything."

Dixie scoffed. "You won't find a better man than Dawson, you know."

Julie smiled. "I know you love Dawson, and I know he's a good man. But, honestly, I'm not sure either of our hearts are ready for a new relationship."

"Well, I'm rooting for both of you!"

"I'm sure you are!" Julie said with a laugh as they pulled into Dixie's driveway.

~

JULIE AND JANINE stood in front of the mirror, each of them putting on their make up. They hadn't done this since they were teenagers, getting ready for dates. It was a familiar scene, although there were quite a few more wrinkles involved and neither of them could get their hair quite as high as they did back in those days.

"So, let me get this straight. You actually had a conversation with William?" Julie asked.

Janine chuckled. "Well, as much of a conversation as you can have with him. He's so prickly, like a porcupine."

Julie brushed through her blonde hair, flipping it side to side, trying to find just the right style for the New Year's eve party. Her sister was so blessed to have thick, curly hair. She could do so many more things with it.

"I know Dawson says he used to be a nice guy, but I just can't see it. Every time I look at him, I just want to smack him across the face."

Janine paused for a moment and then looked at her sister. "I guess I get him a little bit more than most people. He's struggling. There's something going on inside of his brain that is obviously bothering him. I think he just doesn't know how to deal with it."

"I'm glad you're more compassionate than I am about this."

"So, are you excited about your date tonight?" Janine asked, a knowing smile on her face.

"I don't even know if it's a date."

"Oh, please. It's New Year's Eve and he's invited you out. Somebody is going to be smooching before the night is over," she said, giggling and poking her sister in the side.

"Doubtful. I just don't get the feeling that he's going to make that move. Dawson is a very slow mover, and honestly it's probably for the best. Two decades of marriage has really done a number on my brain. Maybe I'm just not ready to move on."

Janine stopped what she was doing and put her hands on her sister's shoulders, both of them looking in the mirror.

"You'll know when you're ready. And Dawson is a catch. The two of you just need to calm down and stop thinking so much. Just let it all happen naturally."

Julie smiled. "When did you become so levelheaded?"

"I think it's the ocean air."

JULIE HADN'T BEEN this nervous in years. Dawson was picking her up any minute, so Janine had gone ahead to the beach. She didn't want to be in the middle of their first date, she said.

When she heard his truck pull up, she peeked out the window. He looked incredibly handsome wearing a pair of jeans, dress boots and a button up white shirt that was untucked.

She opened the door, and his lips immediately formed into a smile. "You look stunning."

Julie had chosen a simple black sundress and a sheer black shawl wrapped around her shoulders. She hoped the night air wasn't going to be too much for her, but tonight fashion had taken precedence over the weather. Since they were going to the beach, she had thought better of wearing high heels and opted instead for a pair of ballet flats. They didn't exactly accentuate the dress, but she didn't want to get stuck in the sand and need to leave her shoes behind.

"Thank you," she said. He pulled a rose from around his back and handed it to her.

"How thoughtful. And roses are my favorite."

"Good. I'm glad I stole it from the neighbor's yard then."

Julie let out a laugh. "Did you really do that?"

"I did. They have plenty. They'll never miss it."

He walked her to his truck and helped her climb inside. As they drove, they chatted about Dixie and the doctor's appointment. Dawson was worried about her just as much as Julie was, and they both decided they were going to keep an eye on William and make sure Dixie had whatever she needed.

When they arrived at the beach, Julie was surprised to see so many cars. People had come from the mainland for the party, but it was unusual to see so many vehicles on the island. It was a little unsettling, and she was glad they would all be going home in a few hours. The island had become her oasis, and she had adjusted to such a slower pace of life. Living in the city seemed foreign to her now.

They walked down to the beach, and she could hear music. There was a dance floor set up with the string lights that looked like something out of a movie. The DJ was playing music from the 80s and 90s, her favorite decades.

"Are you hungry? They usually have a buffet set up over there."

"Who pays for all of this?"

"They sell tickets on the mainland, and those of us who live on the island usually contribute for the catering as well. Local fishermen also donate a lot."

"Nobody asked me to donate. I'll have to make sure to contribute next year."

"Don't worry. They'll hit you up for it soon enough," Dawson said with a chuckle.

They walked around for a while, Dawson introducing her to so many new people. It was great to meet her neighbors. They all seemed like salt of the earth, as her grandmother would say.

"So, I assume Dixie isn't coming tonight?" Dawson asked.

"No. She said that she will leave all of the shenanigans to the young people. She was planning to put her feet up, drink some hot chocolate and watch the last Christmas movies on TV that she had taped. You know she still uses a VCR?"

Dawson laughed. "Why doesn't that surprise me?"

"And with the bookstore closed tomorrow, that will give her a nice long day of rest."

"Listen, Lucy is going to be cooking New Year's dinner tomorrow evening. I hope you and Janine will come. You know, you have to start off the new year with collard greens and black-eyed peas, or else you won't have good luck."

Julie laughed. "Well, I certainly need good luck, so we will be there with bells on."

They both made a plate of food and sat at one of the picnic tables that had been set up temporarily. The two of them spent over an hour talking and laughing, with different residents walking up to introduce themselves to Julie. This place was so unusual. People truly welcomed her there, and everyone seemed happy. She knew they all must have their problems, just like she did, but it was just such a different place. Like something out of an old movie where everybody knew everybody else.

As a kid, she had grown up in a neighborhood a lot like that. At night, she and all the kids in the neighborhood would play spotlight, which was basically just hide and seek in the dark with flashlights. Nobody went home until their parents either rang the dinner bell on their front porch or the street lights came on.

She remembered one time when her mother overreacted because she wasn't home for dinner. She had let time get away from her because she was jumping on a friend's trampoline. Her mom had apparently been calling her from the front porch, but Julie didn't hear her. The next thing she knew, a police patrol car drove up to her friend's house and found her. She remembered being terrified and mad at her mother for sending the police to look for her.

But, that was the way things went in a small town. Everybody knew everybody else, and any parent was basically allowed to discipline any child. She was just as scared of her friends' mothers as she was of her own. You couldn't get away with anything in a tight-knit community like that.

"Man, that was good. I don't think I've ever had salmon marinated like that."

"Yeah, we have some amazing cooks around here. Lucy sent shrimp and grits over, but I didn't even get a scoop. Looks like it's already gone," Dawson said.

"She can definitely cook. That's something I was never really good at. I mean, I cooked for my family, but I'm certainly no gourmet chef."

"Oh, you do all right. Those pork chops you made a few weeks ago are still on my mind."

Julie smiled. "Thanks for saying that, but I know they were just average. Cooking is just not my forte."

"You sell yourself short, Julie."

"Don't we all do that?"

"I guess so. I mean, people tell me I'm good at building things, but I also think I'm just average."

"You're not average."

He looked at her for a long moment. Finally, a slow song came on, and the tension between them started to melt.

"Care to dance?" he asked.

"Of course."

He stood up and reached out his hand, taking hers. They walked to the dance floor, and she slid her arms around his neck as he put his around her waist. As they moved to the music, it felt so familiar and unfamiliar at the same time. She didn't know where to put her head. She wanted to bury it in his chest and suck in the smell of whatever amazing cologne he was wearing. But, she also didn't want to seem too clingy or needy or desperate.

As they swayed, she caught her sister's eye. Janine was smiling and fist pumping in the air. Julie quickly averted her eyes for fear that she would start laughing and ruin the moment.

It reminded her so much of the first time she danced with a boy. She was fourteen years old, and they were at a school dance. Julie had been kind of a wallflower in those years, and she definitely wasn't the most popular girl in school. She sat there on the bleachers in the gym, watching everybody else slow dance, and she felt like the world's biggest loser. Suddenly, a boy a couple of grades older than her that she had a major crush on, walked over and asked her to dance. She knew he was doing it because he felt sorry for her, but she didn't care. She just wanted somebody to want her in that moment.

And, now, she felt the same. She didn't care if Dawson really wanted to have a relationship with her. She just wanted to feel wanted again.

She hadn't realized until now how much she had really missed that feeling, that moment where you realize somebody really wants to be with you. A lot of that gets lost in a marriage, and she had definitely felt that longing even when she was married to Michael. He didn't seem to want her in those last years of marriage. He was there, steady as a rock for a long time. But as she thought back over their marriage, she realized it had been years since she had felt wanted by her husband.

Everything had become mundane. The kids, paying the bills, running errands. They hadn't gone on real dates in several years. Sometimes she blamed herself when she thought about the ways that she had failed in her marriage, wondered if she had pushed him into Victoria's arms.

But then she remembered that they took vows, and that it was his responsibility to be faithful to her no matter what. Every time she thought she was somehow "over" her divorce, she realized that things didn't happen that way. There were stages of grief, even when it came to divorce, and giving herself grace for that was one of the hardest things she'd ever done.

"Are you okay?" Dawson finally asked. She looked up at him.

"Yeah, why?"

"I don't know. You just seemed lost in thought there for a moment."

"I guess I was. But I'm okay. It's going to be a good new year."

"That it is."

They danced to a couple more songs before Julie heard that it was thirty seconds until midnight. The countdown had begun. They walked off the floor, Dawson still holding her hand. Everybody stepped back, watching the countdown on a big monitor they had placed in the corner of the dance floor.

Everybody was laughing, holding up their glasses of champagne or tea. As they counted down 20... 19... 18..., Julie started to feel nervousness in the pit of her stomach. What was she supposed to do? Was the man still responsible for initiating the kiss? Was she supposed to take control as a liberated woman?

Her mind raced more than she ever could've imagined. Why was this so anxiety producing? 12... 11... 10...

Part of her wanted to run. Part of her wanted to turn around and just ask him if he was going to kiss her. Ten seconds seemed way too long to wait to find out the answer.

And just when she was about to explode, 3… 2… 1… And suddenly Dawson's lips were touching hers.

And then everything stopped. Time stopped. The earth wasn't spinning anymore. Even the IRS stopped, and everybody knew they never stopped.

The feel of his warm lips against hers took away all her doubt. He was interested in her, and she was definitely interested in him. And, for now, she was just going to enjoy the feeling of this man who wanted to be with her and not think about all of the future implications. She could do that tomorrow.

CHAPTER 4

Janine sat cross legged in front of the water. Listening to the waves come in and out over and over was comforting to her in a way she couldn't explain. Sometimes, in her deepest meditations, she thought about that day when she was attacked. She went through it again, the trauma still so deep even after months of counseling and group sessions.

The idea of someone overpowering her, taking her choice away, gnawed at her soul. She tried not to truly think about it, but the memories were like wild animals trying to claw their way out of her brain. At least the nightly nightmares had dissipated as she'd become closer to her sister and more comfortable in her new living situation.

There was never talk of her leaving, no conversations about her moving out. She wondered if she and

Julie would live together forever, learning to knit when they got older, and yelling at kids who rode their bikes across the front lawn. That thought made her laugh and feel sad at the same time.

Then, she'd think about seeing Julie and Dawson kiss a few nights before at the New Year's Eve party. Her initial reaction was almost one of jealousy, but not because she was interested in Dawson or mad at her sister. She just wished she had a relationship with a man who loved her, who cared about her well being and only wanted to be with her.

Maybe that was just the stuff of romance novels.

She tried to re-focus her mind as she sat there, but the thoughts kept coming and the seagulls were squawking something fierce. Sighing, she opened her eyes and put on her sunglasses as she took a long sip from her fancy water bottle. Every yogi had to have one.

Off in the distance, she could see William. It had become "their thing" to be at the beach at the same time of morning, but they totally ignored each other. She wondered what was going on in his strange head. Why would anyone treat Dixie poorly? She was the nicest woman Janine had ever met, and many times she'd wondered how cool it would have been to have a mother like her. SuAnn was no Dixie, that much was for sure.

She watched as he stood on his paddle board, staring off into the open ocean. He was steady as a rock, yet his gaze seemed fixed on nothing, as if he was lost in thought.

"What are you looking at?" he yelled. She hadn't noticed him turning to look at her.

"I could ask you the same question," she called back.

A few moments later, he was back on the beach, slowly walking toward her.

"Are you scared?"

"Excuse me?" His comment immediately jarred her for some reason. Her mind raced as she remembered the stranger coming toward her as she walked home that night over two years ago. Like someone replaying a movie, it flashed through her mind, and she could feel the panic coming on. She was alone on a beach with a man she barely knew, and he was walking toward her...

"Hey, are you okay?" he asked, looking at her closely. He reached out to touch her arm, and she stepped back.

"My sister knows I'm here," she said, well aware that Julie was at work.

"What?"

"Don't touch me," she said, her voice shaking. She hated anxiety. It was like an unwelcome visitor when it came on and took over her body.

"I don't now what's going on, but I didn't come over here to hurt you, okay?" His voice was different, reassuring almost. "Just take a few breaths."

She looked at him, and he didn't seem as scary. Janine took in a long, deep breath and then blew it out slowly. As he watched her, concern on his face, she felt really silly.

"I'm sorry about that," she said softly. This was the first time she'd literally panicked right in front of someone. Normally, she ran from the feeling, ducking into public bathrooms if she needed to. Experiencing a panic attack in front of a virtual stranger was one of her biggest fears, and now it had come true.

"No need to apologize. Has this happened before?" Why did he seem like a different person? He was actually worried about her, and that seemed totally out of character.

"Yes, but not as often as it used to."

He dropped his board on the ground and sat down, waving for her to do the same. "Sit. I don't want you to pass out or something."

She sat and looked out at the water. "Why did you ask me if I was scared?"

"I meant were you scared to try stand up paddle boarding. I guess I should have been more specific."

She smiled slightly. "Yeah, maybe don't approach a woman and ask if she's scared? Especially on a deserted beach."

William laughed, and that was something she hadn't expected. "Again, I'm sorry. Are you on edge today or something? I mean, you normally seem kind of chilled out."

Janine smiled. "I've been going to counseling for a few months, and part of what I've learned is that I need to be open about my past in order to overcome it. So, I guess now is as good a time as any. I was attacked a little over two years ago by a stranger when I was living in the Caribbean."

William's face fell, and if it was possible to have no expression, that's what he had. He looked at her for a few impossibly long moments and then finally spoke.

"I had no idea. Of course, you'd freak after what I just did. I truly apologize."

"You couldn't have known. I mean, we haven't even officially met really, other than at Christmas. And I doubt you even remember my name as awkward as that was." She immediately wanted to put her foot in her mouth.

William chuckled. "Yeah, it was pretty awkward. But, I do remember your name. Janine, right?"

"Right. Very good." The anxiety was finally dissipating, and she found herself feeling thankful that someone had been with her in that moment, even if it was William.

"Well, I'm Will, in case you don't remember."

"I thought it was William?"

He smiled. "Only my mother and people who are angry at me call me William."

"Oh, so I guess I should too."

"Hey, I said I was sorry. You're still angry at me?"

She nodded. "Not because of this. Because of your mother."

William sighed and hung his head. "I swear this whole town hates me. My mother should run for office or something. She'd win by a landslide with her fan club."

"Ah, there's your real personality again."

He squinted his eyes at her. "Let's change the subject back to my original question. Are you scared to try paddle boarding?"

"Of course not."

"Good. Tomorrow morning, I'm bringing my extra board. Wear something appropriate, and I'll teach you."

"What makes you think I even want to learn?"

"I've seen you watching me, Janine, and there are only two good reasons for that. Either you want to learn stand up paddle boarding, or you think I'm hot." He sat back on his hands and grinned.

Janine glared at him. "I'll meet you at seven."

DIXIE COULDN'T REMEMBER a time when she felt more nervous. Even though she had seen her son a few times since he abruptly arrived on Christmas

Day, every time she saw him, she seemed to feel more anxious.

A lot had been said between them ten years ago, and it didn't seem that much had changed since that time. William still seemed to be very stuck in his emotions, and, as his mother, it worried her. Of course, she wanted to have a better relationship with him, but she just wanted him to be at peace. He seemed so conflicted, so full of angst.

Since being diagnosed with Parkinson's, more than ever she wanted a relationship with her son. She wanted to spend her final years, whether it was five or twenty of them, with her son by her side. This was her little boy, the child she had raised into a man. She had so many fond memories of him. Teaching him how to ride a bike, baking cookies together at Christmas, taking pictures of him and his girlfriends going to dances in high school.

In recent years, all of that had been snatched away from her. Every time she thought of a happy memory, tears came to her eyes but not because of happiness. Instead, she found herself crying at least a few times a week, thinking about all of the years and memories lost.

At the same time, she was angry at William. He had accused her of not wanting to save his father from the cancer that ravaged his body. Of course, she had talked to Johnny so many times about trying treatments, but her husband was the most stubborn person she had ever known. He didn't want to spend his final days losing his hair and feeling sick. He wanted to spend it with his family, and that's exactly what he did.

When Johnny's funeral was over, William had turned on her. He had been holding in so much anger that she couldn't do something to stop his father from what he perceived as giving up. At first, she felt guilty and really questioned herself as to whether she had done enough. But, she knew in her heart that she had. No amount of explaining that to her son seemed to help, and just a few weeks after his father's death, he left town without a word.

Now, a decade had passed and there was so much water under the bridge. She didn't know how to reconnect with her William. He was a grown man before their relationship had split apart, but now he was much older. She was much wiser. And still, she didn't know what to say or do to make him forgive her for whatever it was he thought she did wrong.

Conflicting emotions were overwhelming, especially given her recent medical diagnosis. She had to find ways to keep her stress under control, and right now that seemed impossible. The more she stressed, the more her tremors acted up. Some days she felt dizzy and tired. And for Dixie, this was the hardest part, not being able to control her body.

She had always been an active woman, both mentally and physically. Now, she struggled many days to work, and with the added stress of her son coming back to town, she felt very defeated.

He had agreed to come over to her house, and she was thankful for that. He said they needed to discuss some things, and she hoped it would be reconciliation. As she peeked out the front window, she saw him pull up and backed away. She didn't want to seem too eager, although she was.

"Hey, son," she said as she opened the door. He nodded slightly, just one side of his mouth going up into into an almost smile.

"Hey." Dixie stepped back and opened the door further, allowing him to come inside. He seemed a little antsy himself, rubbing the palms of his hands down the front of his jeans, something he had done when he was nervous even as a small kid.

"We can sit in the breakfast room," she said. Dixie had the epitome of a southern house, and her breakfast room was one of her favorite places to be. Filled with sunlight and surrounded by windows, it made her feel happy when she sat in there in the mornings drinking her coffee and reading her Bible.

William sat down in one of the plush armchairs Dixie had situated in the bay window. He looked around and slightly smiled.

"Boy, this place hasn't changed much since the last time I was here. Is that Daddy's coffee mug over there?"

Dixie chuckled. "Yes. One of the last times he

drank coffee was out of that mug, and I just couldn't bear to put it away. Even when I donated some of his clothing, I knew I was never going to let go of that mug."

William sighed. "I sure miss that man."

It was the first time she had heard him say anything emotional in so many years. William was one who kept his feelings to himself, so hearing him admit that he missed his father that much was touching to her.

"I know you do. I miss him every day. I put together a really nice photo album, you know, memories and such. I'd love to share it with you sometime."

William nodded slightly. "Yeah, maybe sometime."

"So, what brings you here today?" Dixie asked, unable to handle the suspense any longer.

"Well, I don't know how to say this exactly. I don't want you to think that I'm assuming you're going to kick the bucket anytime soon, because I don't think that. I read a little bit about Parkinson's and I know you can live a long life with it. But, I am concerned about your memory lapses."

"I understand. Julie went with me to the doctor this week, and he told us that those memory problems could be caused by a sleep medication I've been taking for the last few months. He's changed the medication, and we're going to see how I do."

"Julie? You mean the lady whose house we were at on Christmas?"

"Yes. She's like the daughter I never had, that one. She's been so good to me since she moved here a few months ago."

"I see. And so she went to the doctor with you?"

Dixie got the feeling that he was on edge about something. "Yes. She's a good friend."

"I'm your son."

"Of course you are, honey. But I didn't think you would want to go."

William stood up and sucked in a deep breath as he started slowly pacing back-and-forth. "You didn't think your only son would want to go to the doctor with you?"

Dixie sat there, stunned. Her mouth hung open for a moment in disbelief. "William, we haven't exactly had a good relationship for quite some time. Even after you came back here, you've barely spoken two words to me. Why would I think you wanted to go to my doctor's appointment?"

"I came all the way back here, Mom! And you couldn't even ask me? You took some woman that you barely know?"

"Now, that's not fair!" Dixie said, standing up to face him. "Julie isn't just some woman. She's my friend, like a daughter to me now. She and Dawson have helped me so much. I've been here alone for ten years, William. Did you expect that I wouldn't have friends who became like family to me?"

"I know you have friends. But friends should never replace your family."

"No one could replace you. But sometimes friends can be closer than blood relatives. And for ten years, you didn't bother to even check on me. Why did you come back? I don't understand."

There, she finally said it. She truly didn't understand why he came back. Not that she didn't want him to. Of course, she wanted to see her son every day for the rest of her life, but none of this was making any logical sense.

"I came back because… Well, I want to make sure your estate is handled properly."

"My estate? I'm not dead!" Now, she was angry. The Southern spitfire in her was coming out quickly. She stared up at her son, her fire engine red hair well suiting her right now.

William held up his hands. "I know that. I shouldn't have said that. Please, just calm down."

"Son, I love you, but you're very close to getting a smack across the cheek."

William backed up and smiled. "Yes, I remember those."

Dixie took a breath and then laughed. "I only did it twice. Both times you cussed at me, and you know I don't tolerate that."

"Yes, ma'am. I do know that for sure."

They both slowly sat back down and William ran his hands through his dark hair. "I'm not here to cash in, Mom. I just worry that you won't be able to handle the house and the business alone."

"I'm not alone, dear. Don't feel like you have to be somewhere you don't want to be. I've survived all these years alone, and I have my friends."

He rolled his eyes. "Yes, I know about your friends."

"Are you jealous of them?"

"Of course not!"

"Sounds like you are, sweetie. And I just want you to know that I love you more than I could ever love anyone on this planet. But, I won't be mistreated by you or anyone else. I just won't."

He paused for a long moment. "I'm sorry."

"Sorry? For what?"

"For making you feel like I was mistreating you."

She had a choice. She could just accept his apology and try to move on, or she could say what she felt. And it was never in Dixie's nature to keep her words to herself.

"You *have* mistreated me, William. And your father would be very angry at you. I think you would agree." Standing her ground when all she wanted to do was hug her son was hard. But, he needed to understand what he'd done and take responsibility. Mothers never retired, and if she had to teach him a lesson at his age, so be it.

"I was hurt. There's a lot you don't know."

"Then tell me, son. Please."

He considered it for a moment and then shook his head. "It doesn't matter now, and it's not going to change anything. I just want to move on. Can we do that?"

"I don't know. Can we?"

"I'll try if you will."

Dixie forced a smile. "Honey, I never went anywhere. I'm here to be your mother no matter what happens. That will never change."

William looked at his father's mug one more time and then stood. "Good. I think we should just try to move forward. I'd like to be involved in your medical appointments from now on, if that's okay."

Dixie stood. "Of course. Now that I know, you're welcome to come."

"Thank you. I guess I'd better be going. I have to get up early tomorrow."

"New job?"

"No. I've got to teach someone to paddle board." There was a bit of a smile on his face before he turned and walked out the door, leaving Dixie to wonder if her son would ever really hug her again.

CHAPTER 5

*J*ulie looked down at her phone. She had surprisingly good service on the island, which she was thankful for since today Meg had sent her pictures from France. Most of them were her posing in front of various scenes, like a river and a cute little bookstore. Then, toward the end, there were two of her and the man she was dating.

As she stared at his face, she wondered who he really was. Why was he dating someone so much younger? What did he want with her daughter? Was Meg making good decisions?

Her stomach churned as she worried about both of her girls. Colleen seemed to be doing well, and she actually sounded happier on the phone than she ever had. Sometimes, she mentioned her father. Apparently Michael was healing quicker than they

66

expected, and Colleen was happy about that. She was hoping he would visit her when he was better since she had a hard time getting away from work.

Julie had steered clear of asking anything about his relationship with Victoria, and Colleen not mentioning it made Julie believe they had gotten back together. It didn't matter to her anyway. That part of her life was over.

She had started moving on in her life, and all she could do was continue looking ahead. The kiss with Dawson had thrown her for quite a loop and gave her emotions she hadn't expected.

First, she'd felt like her legs were going to come out from under her. Never in her life had she experienced a kiss like that, and that included the one Michael planted on her when they got married. There was just something there she couldn't pinpoint that made her feel like she wasn't standing on solid ground anymore.

More surprising was this sense of guilt she hadn't expected to feel. As a woman who had been married for two decades, it felt strange to kiss another man. She knew it was illogical, and it made her mad at herself for even feeling it, but she did. She tried to give herself grace about it. After all, she wasn't the one who cheated, but she still had to remind herself that it was okay to move on.

And then there was the immediate questioning of what she was doing. Was she moving on too soon?

Was there an appropriate amount of time to wait before getting involved with someone? After all, Michael hadn't died. He had cheated on her. Was she supposed to wait and make sure she wasn't grieving the loss of her marriage before involving someone else?

All of these feelings and ideas had coursed through her body during New Year's dinner with Janine, Dawson and Lucy. It had been a quiet affair, but it felt good to start the new year with people she cared about. Still, it felt like there was some kind of divide between her and Dawson after their kiss, and she wondered if he was having regrets about it.

She turned back to her laptop, which was sitting on her newly purchased deck furniture. One of her favorite things to do was to sit on her deck overlooking the marsh and write on her laptop. She was working on her first novel, a long held dream of hers. The story was similar to her own with a woman her age as the main character. She often found herself welling up with tears as she lived her own story through her character.

"What are you working on?" Janine asked as she walked out onto the deck.

"Becoming a bestselling author," Julie quipped.

"And how's that going?"

"I'm having major writer's block today, for some reason."

Janine sat down across from her and laughed.

"Could it be because you're reliving that kiss from Dawson? Maybe it's boggling your mind." She slid a cup of coffee she'd poured for Julie across the table and then put her own mug to her lips.

"Very funny."

Janine continued grinning. "Come on, it's cute, the two of you."

Julie allowed a smile to creep across her face. "It was pretty nice."

"See? I knew it. Ya'll just looked so... comfortable."

"Comfortable? Is that what I should be going for in a relationship?"

"Well, would you rather be uncomfortable?" Janine asked, cocking her head.

"No. I just don't know how to feel."

"Why? I thought you liked Dawson?"

Julie put her hands on the sides of her mug to warm up. Evenings on the marsh were cooler in January. "I do. I just don't know... is it too soon? Should I be alone for awhile before I start something with a new man?"

"You aren't required to have a waiting period, Julie. You're an adult, and maybe you just happened to meet the perfect guy quicker than you thought. Are you going to give that up just because it happened sooner than you thought it would?"

"I didn't say I was giving up. I'm just going to go by how I feel and take it step-by-step."

"Fine. But, I think you two make the world's cutest couple, so I am definitely pro Julie and Dawson."

"Duly noted. Now, why don't you come inside and help me clean up the kitchen? You avoid doing dishes like you did when we were kids."

Janine laughed. "Why change what works?"

"Come on, I'm going to show you how to scrub a stained pot."

Julie stood up and Janine followed behind her. "Oh, goody. I can't wait. But, we have to finish up early because I need to go to bed earlier tonight."

Julie stopped and turned around. "Go to bed? Do you have somewhere important to be tomorrow?"

Janine smiled. "I'm going to learn how to stand up paddle board in the morning."

"And who is going to teach you this?"

"William."

Julie's eyes widened. "William? As in Dixie's son?"

"The very one."

"Why on earth would you want to spend any time with that jerk?"

"I think there's more to him than meets the eye."

"Maybe so, but it's not your responsibility to hang around with him."

"Julie, you forgave me after all those years. And the people in my support group gave me grace and help when I didn't deserve it. I was pretty prickly when I started going to those meetings. Don't you think somebody should give William a chance?"

"I suppose so, but watch yourself. I think he came back to town for his own selfish reasons."

"Duly noted," Janine said as Julie handed her a dishcloth and pointed at the sink full of dishes.

JANINE STOOD ON THE BEACH, the early morning sun barely enough to keep the chill off her skin. She wondered about her sanity when she thought of how much colder the water was going to be. Never one to shrink from a challenge, she wasn't about to let on that she was cold. William already thought she was "weak", and she definitely didn't want anyone to perceive her that way.

But he wasn't even there yet. It was seven o'clock right on the dot, and Janine was chronically punctual. She looked around, not wanting to appear too eager if he happened to be walking up behind her, but she saw no one. Maybe he was playing a trick on her, although she couldn't figure out what his reasoning would be.

Just when she was about to give up hope that he was coming and settle in for her regular yoga and meditation practice, she saw him walking up out of the corner of her eye. True to his word, he was holding two boards.

"Glad you could join me," Janine said with a sarcastic smile.

"Takes a little longer when you're walking with two large boards and two long paddles. Cut me some slack. I'm here."

"Sorry. I thought maybe you were ditching me."

"Sensitive much?"

"Maybe this was a bad idea," Janine said, turning toward her mat.

"No, it's not. Come on. I was just messing with you."

She put her hand on her hip and glared at him. "You know, it's hard to tell when you're messing around with that sourpuss look on your face all the time."

"Ouch. Can we start over?"

She smiled slightly. "Fine. Good morning, William. How are you this morning?"

"I'm super fantastic, Janine. How about yourself?" he asked, with a big fake grin on his face.

"I'm doing well. Shall we do some stand up paddle boarding?"

To her surprise, William actually laughed. "That was really awkward. Maybe we can find a happy medium?"

"Sounds good. So, tell me about this stick thingy," Janine said, reaching out and taking one of the poles from his hand.

"Um, that would be your paddle."

"Right." She looked at it up and down. It was a lot taller than she was.

"So, the first thing we need to do is adjust the height of the pole. You're a little…"

"Short?"

"I was going to say miniature, but short's fine."

"Very funny."

He smiled again, and she realized he wasn't bad looking when he didn't look like an angry wolverine.

Walking closer, he unclamped something on her pole and started adjusting the height downward. He reached for her arm and held it in the air, bent it and then locked the pole again. "There. You want it about as high as your arm when it's slightly bent."

"Got it."

"Now, let's talk about what you're going to do when you get the board out in the water. We have to get it to the calmer areas, so we'll have to swim out, climb on and stand up."

"Okay."

He laid the two boards down, side by side, and knelt on his. "First, you want to start in this kneeling position. Lay your pole across like this. It'll give you more balance. Once you're ready to stand up, put one foot in front like this…"

He showed her how to stand up, and she climbed on her own board to mimic what he'd done.

"Seems simple enough."

William chuckled. "That's because you're on dry land."

"Are you saying I won't be able to do this?" she asked, her hand on her hip again.

"I'm just saying prepare to eat some water the first few times."

"Wow, not a very reassuring teacher, Will."

He paused for a moment. "Huh."

"Huh what?"

"Oh, nothing. It's just weird to hear you call me Will."

"I'm not a very formal person, but if you'd prefer that I call you William…"

"No, I like it," he said, not making eye contact. "Okay, so let's keep going."

For the next few minutes, he continued explaining how to maneuver the paddle board. He told her how to hold the paddle and to make sure to do five to seven strokes on each side before switching. He showed her where to stand, slightly in front of the middle unless she wanted to turn, in which case she needed to step back a bit so that the front of the board would come up out of the water slightly. And, when she was turning, she was supposed to push her paddles from back to front.

It was a lot to remember. But, the last thing she was going to do was be shown up in front of Will. Weakness was not the way she wanted to be perceived by anyone, but especially not this guy. For some reason, he just got under her skin.

"So, are we ready to take them out on the water?" she asked.

He smiled. "Do you think you're ready?"

"Are you?" she said, enjoying their banter.

"Let's go then."

She followed him to the water's edge and they each swam out into the water, pulling their paddle boards behind them until they found calmer waters. Getting up onto the paddle board was difficult, and probably not the best way to go about things. Normally, people did this sort of thing in a nice, calm bay or a lake. Of course, Janine had to find the most difficult circumstance to learn.

Surprisingly, she was able to get up on her board and maintain her balance, probably due to all those years of intense yoga training. William looked impressed.

They paddled around, sometimes near each other and sometimes further away. Eventually, they were able to line up their boards and have bits of conversation as they moved along. Janine really enjoyed seeing different parts of the island, but she did worry she wouldn't be able to get back to the beach they started from.

"So, how long have you been doing this?" she asked.

"Several years. I was living close to the water,

near a lake, and a friend of mine taught me how to do it. It's a lot easier in the lake than it is in the ocean, but I like the challenge."

"Yeah, I like challenges too. Speaking of that, have you talked to your mother lately?"

He laughed slightly. "That was quite a segue."

"Thank you. I pride myself on my conversational skills. Anyway, answer the question."

"Yes. I saw her yesterday. Visited her at her home. We had a nice talk. I told her that I would like to come to her doctor appointments."

"Let me guess. She told you that Julie came and that made you a wee bit jealous?"

"Not jealous. I just don't understand why she's dragging an almost stranger to her doctor appointments instead of her only son."

Janine glared at him. "Julie is my sister and not a complete stranger. She and Dixie work together, and they are very close friends. They have helped each other through some tough times these last few months."

"Look, I know she's your sister and I don't want to get into a whole argument about this. But my mother's health should be my concern and no one else's."

"I'm sorry, but I don't think that's true. When you abandoned your mother, she was forced to create a whole new network of people to help her as she has gotten older. It seems to me that that is on you."

He stopped paddling and stood there on his board. Janine was afraid he would lose his balance and topple into the water, and she was definitely not strong enough to pull him back up .

"Maybe you're right. It probably is my fault that she was forced into making new friends. But I'm here now, and I want her to treat me like her son again."

Janine stopped and sat down on her board to take a break. A few moments later, Will followed behind.

"Look, I know what it's like to be estranged from your family. Julie and I didn't talk for many years either. She was mad at me, I was mad at her. Our crazy mother was in the middle. It was a whole ordeal. But, you can fix this. The key is taking responsibility for your part, and it just doesn't seem like you're doing that."

"No offense, but you don't know anything about me or my relationship with my mother. It's not like we're friends or anything. I just offered to teach you how to stand on a paddle board."

Janine could tell he was closing himself off. He was getting defensive, and nothing good was accomplished when someone got defensive.

"Right. I realize we're not friends. And it's none of my business, but thankfully I have you trapped in the ocean with no way to get out of here quickly. So you're going to listen to me."

He smiled slightly. "Has anyone ever told you that you're a little bit abrasive, blunt and nosy?"

"Yes. Anyway, don't try to distract me. I would like to give you a little piece of unsolicited advice. And that advice is that you need to forgive your mother for whatever it is you think she did and show her that you love her. Not that you're here to take over her business or her life or her money. But that you just want to be here because she's your mom and you've missed her. If you can't do that, honestly, you should just go. Dixie is dealing with a lot right now, and added stress is one of the worst things you could put on her already overflowing plate."

"I appreciate your input."

Janine stared at him for a moment. "That's all you have to say?"

"Yes, because I don't want to aggravate a woman who could push me off of this board and leave me stranded out in the middle of the ocean."

"Smart guy."

They both stood back up on their boards and started paddling again, this time turning back toward the beach. Turning was a little bit more diffi-cult than Janine had imagined, and before she knew it, she leaned too much to the right and toppled straight into the water. It was freezing! Even though it was in the mid 60s outside, the water felt like she was going to freeze into a popsicle in less than a minute.

"Are you okay?" Will asked as he circled back and came over to where she was.

"Well, I've been better. Right now, I know what an ice cube feels like."

"Here, let me help you," he said, reaching down into the water and pulling her up onto his board. Never had she been so thankful to be out of the water, but now she was even colder with the ocean winds assaulting her body.

"I know you must be freezing, so let's get you to shore as quickly as we can. I think I have a blanket in my truck."

"Thanks," she said, feeling very safe with him for some reason. Nobody in town liked William right now, but she didn't find him to be so bad. She saw good in him, and maybe someday other people would too.

He helped her get back onto her board and back up onto her feet so that they could paddle to shore. It seemed to take forever. She was freezing down to her bones.

When they arrived on shore, she dragged her paddle board onto the sand and then sat down before laying down onto her back. Thankfully, the sun was starting to beat down a bit, slowly warming her body back up to a normal temperature. Will ran to his truck and came back with a plush blanket, wrapping it around her shoulders as he sat down beside her.

"Thanks for helping me."

"Of course. What did you think I would do? Wave goodbye and say good luck being shark bait?"

She laughed. "I think sometimes you put on this male bravado exterior, but you're really just a nice guy at heart."

He blew out a breath. "Everyone has a right to their own opinion."

"Why is it that you don't want people to think you're nice?"

"You know, I think you might have missed your calling. You'd make a great therapist. I wouldn't come to see you, but I'm sure somebody would like to answer all of your questions."

Janine laughed. "Fine. I guess learning to paddle board was enough for today. But, since I tried your thing, why don't you meet me here in the morning at seven and try mine?"

"You mean yoga? No thank you."

"Are you scared?"

"Of course not. It just looks kind of silly, if you ask me."

She rubbed her hands together and let out an evil laugh. "Oh, if you only knew how many people have said that to me and then ended up in a puddle on the floor, including my own sister."

"I just don't see the need to fold myself into a bunch of weird poses."

"Which is exactly why you need it. I tried your thing, and you can try mine."

"You realize I can say that I'll be here but I don't have to actually show up."

"Fine. I'll be here at seven in the morning regardless. I hope you'll join me." She stood up and handed him his blanket. "Thanks for teaching me a new skill today. I'll see you in the morning."

Before he had a chance to say anything else, she was at the pathway and headed back home.

CHAPTER 6

*D*awson sat at the dining room table and stared down at his pancakes. He was hungry, but had no appetite at the same time. His dreams had been keeping him up all night for the last week, and he just didn't know what to do about it.

His late wife kept coming to him in dreams, although she never said anything. She was always just out of reach, looking at him with an ethereal white light around her. She wasn't smiling, but she wasn't angry. She was just there.

Since his kiss with Julie on New Year's Eve, he had felt so conflicted. He was very interested in her, and could honestly see himself getting serious. But there was this part of him that felt so guilty like he was wiping away the life he had with Tania. Like she and his child didn't exist or didn't matter anymore.

He didn't know what to do. He didn't know whether to pursue Julie and just try to push those feelings to the back of his mind, or whether it was even fair to drag Julie into a relationship where he still felt such an attachment to his wife.

"Something wrong with the pancakes?" Lucy asked as she walked into the dining room.

"No, of course not. You make the world's best pancakes, after all."

"My mama made the world's best pancakes. I'm a close second."

Dawson laughed. "Just another long night."

"What's going on, honey?" She was like a mother to him, and he really wished his own mother or grandmother was there right now. He missed them so much, especially when he needed life advice.

"It's Tania. I've been having dreams."

"Ohhh. I get it now. You've seemed kind of blue lately. I couldn't put my finger on what was going on."

"I just keep seeing her. She's just staring at me. And now, you know I've been spending some time with Julie."

Lucy sat down and reached across the table, putting her hand on top of his. She smiled that reassuring smile. "Sweetie, Tania was a good woman. She loved you with all her heart, and I know you loved her also. But she'd want you to be happy and move on."

"Do you really think so?"

"Of course. She wouldn't want you to live your whole life alone. She wasn't that kind of person. Plus, maybe she sent Julie to you. Ever think about that?"

"No, I hadn't thought of that. I just don't know how to feel. I guess it'll take some time."

"True. No need to rush anything. Enjoy the ride, I always say." She stood and wiped down he table with a dish towel.

"Enjoy the ride. Good advice, Lucy."

JULIE STARED OFF INTO SPACE, trying to think of the next line of her book. She was just to the part where the husband tells the wife that he's cheating on her. It was taking everything in her to write this part, as it hit so close to home. She felt tears one minute and insane amounts of rage the next.

"Excuse me. Do you have any books about organic gardening?" a woman asked. Julie hadn't even heard her come in. She quickly closed her laptop and smiled.

"Of course. They are right over there in that section on the left, next to the red bookshelf."

"Thank you," the woman said with a grateful smile before walking to the other side of the store.

She opened her laptop again and started to type.

The words were just starting to flow again when her cell phone rang in her pocket. She closed her laptop again and answered.

"Hello?"

"Hey, Mom!" Colleen said, cheerfully.

"Hey, honey. So good to hear your voice. I know you've been busy lately with your cases, but I was worried you'd forgotten your old mom."

Colleen laughed. "Never. I've just been so busy. And I have some big news, Mom."

"News?"

"Yes. I'm coming for a visit!"

"To Seagrove?"

"Yep! I'll be there next week! Hope you have some extra room for me... and a friend."

"A friend?"

"Okay, my boyfriend, Peter."

Julie paused for a moment. "You have a boyfriend?"

"I know I haven't said anything, but that's because I wanted to make sure this was a serious thing."

"How long have you been dating?"

"Six months."

"Six months?" Julie shrieked. "And you didn't tell me? What is going on with my girls?"

"What do you mean?"

"Meg is in love, you're in love, and nobody told me?"

"Mom, in fairness, you've had a rough few months. We thought it was best to not overwhelm you with things."

"Honey, knowing my daughters are happy and in love would've been a blessing. You can always tell me anything."

"I know, and I'm sorry. But I can't wait for you to meet Peter. He's so wonderful, Mom. He's an attorney in a firm I interviewed with a few months ago. We met in an elevator, like in some sappy romance movie. Anyway, I didn't get the job, but I got the guy!"

"I'm happy for you, sweetie. And I can't wait to meet him. I'll set up the guest room for you, and we have a pull-out sofa in the living room for Peter."

There was silence for a moment. "Mom, Peter and I already live together."

"What?"

"I know you don't like it, but we got an apartment together several weeks ago."

"Oh."

Julie had been raised in a conservative home, and living together wasn't at all what she envisioned for her daughter. But, she also realized Colleen was an adult, and she could make her own decisions. It was so hard to straddle the line of letting her live her life and still trying to parent her.

"Mom, we're happy, so I hope you can accept him."

"Of course, I will, Colleen. It's just a lot to take in. I'm sure Meg has told you about her new beau?"

"Yes, I've known for awhile, and I know you don't approve of his age."

"Not really, but you two are adults now, and I just have to trust your decisions. But, it doesn't mean I'm going to like all of them."

"I know, I know," Colleen said with a laugh. "We'll fly in mid week, so we'll just take a rental car to your house."

"Don't you want me to pick you up at the airport?"

"No, it's fine. We'll see you soon!"

"I can't wait!"

Julie was looking forward to seeing her daughter. It had been so long. She sure hoped she liked this Peter fellow or things were going to get awkward really fast.

JANINE STOOD tall on her yoga mat as she reached straight up into the sky. She swept her arms down and fell forward, her head hanging and stretching her back in the best way. She loved yoga, and every day she did it, she was thankful to have learned it so many years ago. It had changed her life, even saved her life, several times.

Still, this morning she wasn't totally at peace. She

wondered if Will was going to show up. She truly believed she could help him get over the anger he felt at his mother, and probably his father too, by showing him how to go inward for answers and comfort. But, if he didn't show up and do the work, she couldn't help him.

Opening her yoga business in a few weeks was going to be a challenge, but she was excited about the prospect of helping so many people and being able to do it on the beautiful beaches of Seagrove. This place was her home, and she hoped to never leave it. Her big dream was to make enough money to buy her own little house on the island because she didn't want to impose on her sister forever.

She moved into warrior pose and stood strong and stable, staring out at the vast water. This pose always made her feel so powerful, which was its intention. As she released the pose, she could feel someone nearby and turned around to see William standing there.

"Good morning. I didn't think you'd come," she said.

He shrugged his shoulders. "Turnabout is fair play, I guess."

"True. So, I brought an extra yoga mat for you." She reached down and handed him a rolled up blue mat. "You can roll it out right next to me here."

He tossed the mat out in front of him and rolled it out with his foot. Janine could tell he wasn't totally sold on this idea, but at least he was there, and that was half the battle.

"Before we start doing yoga, I'd like to show you how to meditate." Janine sat down on her mat, cross legged, and looked up at him.

"That's bait and switch." He sat down and leaned back on his hands, his legs stretched out in front of him.

"Will, meditation is key to getting the most out of yoga. At least try it, okay?"

"I'm not really that kind of person."

"What kind of person is that?"

"A calm person who can just clear their mind and forget everything that is going on in life."

Janine started laughing. "Do you think that's the kind of person I was when I started meditating? Of course not! Meditation is to quiet the mind. When I started, I was a wreck. I had so much going on in my life, and I couldn't manage. That's why I started meditating in the first place."

"I just don't know if I am the sort of person who's going to be able to quiet my mind. There's a lot going on in there."

Janine smiled. "I have hope for you. But you have to try. Give it your best shot."

"Fine. I'll try. So what do we do. Sit crosslegged and chant?"

"Very funny. Sit up straight, and cross your legs. Close your eyes and just start taking in some deep breaths. In through your nose, and out through your mouth. Hold your breath for just a second or two at the top."

William readjusted and sat up, crossing his legs and facing the ocean. To her surprise, he immediately closed his eyes and started breathing in and out just as she had said. She watched him for a moment, and it occurred to her that he looked so different when he was vulnerable.

"Continue breathing in and out, and I want you to try to keep your mind clear. If any thoughts flow into your mind, don't judge them. Don't be harsh with yourself. Simply push them away and keep a blank slate. Concentrate on your breath only." She watched him for several minutes as he breathed in and out. His face changed, and he looked more peaceful.

Eventually, she re-situated herself onto her mat and joined him in the breathing. For a good fifteen minutes, they breathed in and out together, almost in unison at times. The only sound was the ocean waves in front of them and their breath flowing in and out of their bodies.

Finally, Janine spoke. "Okay, so we're going to take one final deep breath in and hold it for three seconds and then blow it out. And when you blow it out, imagine you are blowing away all of your stress and negativity."

When they were finished, William slowly opened his eyes, shielding them from the sun.

"Well, what did you think?" Janine asked.

He smiled slightly. "That wasn't so bad."

"Oh really? Coming from you, that's a rousing seal of approval."

"Actually, I can see why you like it. I feel a lot calmer."

"Good. That's what we were going for. Now, I'm really going to challenge you. Your body is calm, your mind is centered, and now it's time to show you what yoga can do for you."

"I'm a little scared," he said. "Don't twist me into a pretzel or anything."

Janine bumped her shoulder into his. "Yoga is fun. It's not a competition. You just do your best, and let me do the rest."

"I don't know why, but I trust you."

For some reason, that made her feel good. He was starting to trust her, and she was pretty sure he didn't trust people easily. Maybe that boded well for her abilities as a teacher.

"Okay, so stand up. We're going to start with mountain pose."

William stood up, and Janine spent the next few minutes taking him slowly through a series of poses that would be suitable for a beginner. He had challenges along the way, but she could tell he was really trying.

When they finally got to the end, they laid on their backs and stared up into the blue sky. He didn't say anything for a few moments, probably because she had instructed him to be quiet and go inward. But, after a while, he finally spoke.

"I think I just stretched muscles that I didn't even know I had."

Janine chuckled. "I can't tell you how many times people have told me that."

"But, it's good. I mean it's a good feeling. It's different than when I paddle board or run. It's like I have this strange energy moving through my body now."

"That's your Chi."

"My what?"

"It's your life force. We all have that inside of us, but we let things block it up. It's kind of like a clogged drain."

"Well, that was a nasty metaphor."

"Maybe, but accurate."

"Okay, so I'll play along. What kinds of things block our Chi?"

"Life, in a nutshell. All of the bad things that happen to us, or more accurately, the way we react to them. Anger, frustration, holding grudges."

"Well, then mine should be pretty blocked up. I might need professional assistance getting my drain unclogged."

She looked over and smiled at him. "This was a great first step."

They sat there silently for a few minutes, staring out over the water. She could tell he was still trying to catch his breath and use his legs again. Yoga had a tendency to wear out the legs.

"So, paddle boarding tomorrow?" he asked, not making eye contact.

"Yoga and meditation afterward or before?"

He glanced over at her and then stared back at the ocean. "I think we better do it afterward. I'm not sure I'll be able to stand up on my board after this."

She laughed. He stood up, rolled up his mat and handed it to her.

"I'll see you in the morning," she said.

William smiled slightly, nodded his head and walked away. What was this? A new friendship? Something more? She had no idea, but after the last two years she'd had, she felt like she was required to extend an olive branch to this guy since nobody else in town seemed to want him there.

JULIE WAS LITTLE BIT NERVOUS. Dixie had asked to meet her at a local restaurant which wasn't something she commonly did. Usually, they had all of their chats drinking coffee outside of the bookstore. But today, they had closed a little early to do inventory and then Dixie had asked to meet her later for an early supper.

As she sat by the water, sipping on her sweet tea and munching on bread, she stared out at a group of birds flying overhead. This place was magical. All of the wildlife, the scenery and even the people made her feel like it was the one thing she had been missing her whole life.

She turned to see Dixie walking up to the table, a broad smile on her face. She seemed to have been doing better in recent days, especially since the doctor had changed her sleep medicine. Not only was she sleeping better, but she said her memory was improving. Julie hoped she was right about that.

"Hey there!" Dixie said as she sat down. The waitress immediately walked over and took her drink order before disappearing into the building.

"Hello, yourself. Don't you look pretty this evening?" Julie said. Dixie had changed clothes and was wearing a pair of red flowy pants and a lightweight black cardigan. Of course, she also had on all of her requisite jewelry. Dixie was a sharp dresser and didn't care what anybody thought about her sense of style.

"Thank you. I'm actually going to a book club meeting tonight. I haven't been to one in so many months, and I miss some of my old lady friends."

"You're not an old lady!" Julie said, waving her hand.

"Oh, yes I am. And I'm okay with it. I don't say that as a put down. I like being old. People think I'm wise, even if I'm not."

"Well, I think you're pretty wise. But I am a little curious as to why you invited me here tonight, especially if you have someplace else you need to be.

"I have something important I wanted to talk to you about, and I wanted to make sure we didn't get interrupted."

"Okay. You're scaring me a little bit."

"No, I think this is a good thing. "

"All right, what's going on?"

Dixie took in a deep breath, leaned down and pulled some papers out of her large handbag.

"I spoke with my attorney yesterday. He drew up some papers for me. Having Parkinson's, it has made me think more about my business and what I'm going to leave behind one day."

"Don't talk like that, Dixie. The doctor said you're going to have a long, productive life."

"And I believe I am. You can't squash an old bird like me!"

"I like how you think, even though I don't like the picture of someone squashing a bird."

Dixie cackled, which warmed Julie's heart. She has been so sad in recent days, but her emotional state seemed to be getting better. "Anyway, you've become like a daughter to me. And you know how to run the bookstore almost better than I do. There's going to come a time when I want to relax a little bit more."

"Of course. I told you I can work as many hours as you need."

"Well, you see, that's just it. I don't want you to just be an employee. I want you to be my partner."

Julie was stunned. Her mouth was hanging open so much that she was afraid spit was going to drop right onto the table in front of her. "What?"

"You heard me. Your ears are younger than mine!"

"Yes, I heard you, but are you sure about this? I mean, you haven't known me that long. And I don't... I don't want to take part of your business away from you..."

"Julie, I'm not mentally unstable. I know what I want, and I want you to be my business partner. When something happens to me, my part of the business will go to you. You will have earned it. The changes you've made to the store have resulted in more sales already, and I just feel comfortable with you there."

"Dixie, I'll be there no matter what. You don't have to give me half of the business to keep me around. You're going to have a hard time getting rid of me no matter what you do!"

Dixie smiled. "I want to do this. So, will you become my partner?"

Julie giggled. "I feel like you're proposing marriage to me."

"Well, no, I prefer a tall, dark and handsome man. Sorry."

"Same here."

"So what do you say? Are you ready to dive into this crazy business with me? "

"Yes, I am!" Julie said excitedly.

"Well, sweetie, sign here on the dotted line!"

She slid the papers across the table and handed Julie a pen. This was getting real. It looked like Seagrove was going to be her home for a long time to come.

CHAPTER 7

*W*illiam stared at his mother. "You did what?"

"Look, honey, I know this might be upsetting to you. But, Julie has been working with me for months now, and she knows the business."

"Mom, it's a bookstore. It can't be that hard."

Dixie glared at her son. "Now, you listen to me. Down Yonder has been my baby for decades. It has been hard to keep it in business that long, and I'm getting tired of working so much."

"So, hire more help. Why would you give half of your business away?"

"Because it's mine to give, William."

He sighed. "I know that, Mom. It's just that… well, if I'm being honest, it feels like you're replacing me with this Julie woman."

Dixie smiled and rubbed his arm. "Nobody could

replace my only son. And I'm leaving this place to you when I kick the bucket, so you'll still be inheriting something great," she said, stretching her arms out. They were standing in her kitchen, a pot of coffee brewing on the counter beside them.

"I don't want your money, Mom."

"Well, good, because I'm not leaving this Earth any time soon, unless the good Lord decides to snatch me out of here before I'm ready to go!"

William chuckled. "Your personality sure hasn't changed much over the years."

"Nope, not a lick. Now that my doctor has me on some happy pills, I finally feel myself coming back. Sure, I still have symptoms that bother me, but I'm feeling better. And I sure am glad my baby boy has come home. How's the job hunt going?"

"I got an offer yesterday, actually. A firm over in Charleston."

"That's great, sweetie! Are you going to take it?"

"I think so. The pay is great, and I could keep my new apartment here. It's only a short drive."

"I'm so happy for you, William. You seem so much happier lately too. Have you also been to my doctor?" she joked. His mother had always been the funniest person he knew.

"No, but I have been doing yoga and meditating."

She stared at him, her eyes wide. "*My* son has been meditating? What on Earth?"

William laughed. "Yeah, Janine dared me, and

we've been taking turns teaching each other for the last week or so. I've been showing her how to stand up paddle board, and she's been teaching me yoga and meditation."

"Wow. I never saw that coming."

"Neither did I, but I actually enjoy it. Well, for the most part. She's a tough teacher, and I've pulled a few muscles this week." He reached around the back of his thigh and rubbed it.

"I bet. I know her classes start soon. I think she'll do really well around here."

"Yeah, she's a nice person." His face started to flush, part of his Irish ancestry that he despised. He turned and poured a cup of coffee.

"Hmmm. Looks like you might have a little crush?"

"No, Mom. Let's not start false rumors."

"Aw, now, those are the best kind!"

He poured another mug and slid it in her direction. "Here, drink your coffee and fill up that gossiping mouth of yours."

Dixie cackled and pinched her son on the arm.

JULIE STOOD in her kitchen and stared at the floor. It was filled with at least an inch of water, some of it starting to fill her living room too. She had already texted Dawson to come take a look, something she did any time a house related issue came up. Sometimes, she felt bad calling him over, but he was the only contractor on the island and she tried to pay him every time. Most of the time, he refused her money.

She grabbed as many towels as she could find, most on her sister's bathroom floor - some things never changed - and started sopping up as much water as she could. Janine had gone into town to finalize her business license, leaving Julie with the task of cleaning up the wet mess.

"Yikes, you weren't kidding," Dawson said as he walked through the front door.

"Yeah, not a good thing to come home to after work. I don't know what happened."

"Let me take a look," he said, going into the kitchen and starting to poke around under the cabinets. Within a few minutes, he had isolated the issue. "Dishwasher."

"The dishwasher?"

"Yeah, there's a leak back here..." He tried to show her, but Julie didn't have a clue what he was talking about. Still, she nodded along.

"Can you fix it?"

"Yeah, I think I have what I need on my truck."

Dawson went out and rummaged around in his truck before returning to the kitchen. She watched him as he fell right into his zone. When he was working on something, he was completely focused on it, even if it meant laying in a few inches of water on her brand new kitchen floor.

He fiddled around for awhile before finally proclaiming victory. He stood up and laughed as he looked at his soaking wet clothes.

"I wish I could say I had clothes you can wear, but I don't exactly wear your size," Julie said.

"No problem. I'll worry about that when I get home. Let me grab my Shop Vac from the truck and get this water cleaned up. I'll have you all fixed up in no time."

"How about I cook you some dinner after you finish? I have some chicken I can pop in the oven."

"That actually sounds really good. Plus, we haven't gotten to catch up in a few days. I'm anxious to hear about that meeting you had with Dixie."

"You won't believe what happened," Julie said, giving him a little tease of her big news.

When Dawson finished fixing the leak, he sucked up all of the water from the kitchen as Julie did her best to use towels to clean up the baseboards. She was thankful to have hardwood floors and tile rather than carpet right now.

Once they were convinced everything was cleaned up, she popped some chicken into the oven and put some potatoes on to boil so she could make mashed potatoes.

"Want to have a cup of coffee on the deck while we wait for dinner cook?" she asked.

"Sure. That sounds good."

She poured two cups of coffee and they went outside to sit down. The sun had already set, leaving only bits of orange and purple in the night sky as the blackness started to overtake it. The marsh was beautiful any time of day, but she particularly enjoyed the sunsets. Often, the sky looked like artwork someone had painted especially for her. She was thankful to God in those situations, because had her life not been turned upside down by Michael, she might never have been witness to such a beauty.

"So, tell me this amazing news from Dixie. Did she get an update on her treatment plan?"

"No, but she's doing a lot better on her new medication and therapy regimen. I can really see a difference in her."

"Good. I'm so glad. I have been so worried about her. So, if it's not that, then what did she say?"

"Well, to my complete shock, she asked me to be her partner at the bookstore. We signed papers and everything."

Dawson's mouth dropped open. "Seriously? That's amazing, Julie! I'm so happy for you. I'm sure William is going to lose his mind over that, though."

"Probably. I'm expecting a visit from him any time now."

"He won't come here. He's not that stupid. He knows I would wipe the floor with him if he did something like that."

Julie smiled. "Well, thanks for being my personal bodyguard, but I think I could handle him."

"Of course, you could. Sorry. Sometimes my southern chivalry gets the best of me."

"No, it's fine. It feels nice to have someone being protective over me for a change."

They sat silently for a few moments, drinking their coffee and staring out over the water. As the moon took its place in the sky overhead, glimmers of white light shone down on the water, giving the appearance of thousands of diamonds reflecting off of it.

"Can we talk about something?" Dawson finally asked. Out of all the men she had ever met, Dawson was much more prone to talking about his feelings than any of them.

"Sure. What's up?"

"Our kiss... On New Year's eve ..."

She smiled, grateful for the darkness as the redness creeped up in her cheeks. "What about it?"

He took another sip of his coffee and then set it on the table between them. "It was nice, don't you think?"

She laughed. "Yes, I think it was very nice."

"But did it feel kind of... strange to you?"

"I don't know if I would call it strange. It just felt... different. You know, I haven't kissed anyone else in over twenty years. Of course, I didn't think my husband had either, but it seems he did."

Dawson chuckled and then stopped himself. "Sorry. I know that's not funny."

"It is. I was making a joke, so it's okay. But, it did make me feel almost like I was cheating. There's just this part in my mind that still feels like a married woman."

"I understand. My wife has been gone all these years, and I felt the same way. I really haven't dated since she died. And then I keep seeing her in dreams, and I just think it has made me feel so conflicted and guilty."

"I'm so glad you said something because I felt really silly having these thoughts. Maybe we just need to take things slowly. What do you think?"

"For us, maybe. I'm kind of a slow mover as it is, but I just don't want to screw this up. I know you still have some healing to do after your divorce, and I'm thinking maybe I still have healing to do that I didn't realize."

"I hope you don't get offended when I say this, but maybe you could go see a counselor about it. I know grief can be something that sticks, and it's hard to get over. Maybe you just need to talk it out with somebody."

He sat quietly for a moment. "Maybe. I'll think about it."

"Just do whatever is best for you, Dawson. If all we ever have is this amazing friendship, I will consider myself blessed." Even as she said it, she knew she didn't totally mean it. What she really wanted was a relationship with him. She saw herself, thirty years down the road, still looking into his eyes. But she wasn't about to say that and scare him off.

"I only want the best for you too. I think maybe we just take it slow and see where it goes."

"I agree," she said, wishing like crazy that relationships were easier after divorce. Maybe it would start getting better, or maybe she'd end up an old maid, feeding alligators down by the marsh and knitting little muzzles for them.

"GOOD MORNING," William said as he rolled out the yoga mat next to Janine and sat down. This had become their tradition, him showing up at 7 AM with two coffees in his hands, and Janine teaching him how to use meditation to quiet his mind. Sometimes they would also paddle board, depending on how cold it was. Other times, she showed him increasingly difficult yoga poses.

It was weird, but comfortable. Sometimes, she didn't know what to think about this guy. He was still abrasive, at times, but he seemed to be loosening up in a way that she had not expected.

"Good morning."

He handed her the cup of coffee, which was actually a vanilla latte from the coffee shop on the mainland, and they stared out over the water.

"So, I found out something recently."

"Oh yeah? What?"

"My mom gave half of her business to your sister."

Janine had figured this was coming, and she honestly didn't know what she was going to say when it finally came up. On the one hand, she could understand how he might be offended that his mother would give half of her business to Julie. But, on the other hand, given their track record, she could totally see why Dixie would make that choice.

Of course, she was also immensely happy for her sister to have the opportunity. Julia worked hard at the bookstore, and she deserved something new in her life.

"And how do you feel about that?"

"Well, to be honest, at first I was really ticked off. I didn't even let on to my mother how upset I was because I didn't want to destroy the progress that we've made. But, I did some meditating on it last night, and I feel at peace with it now."

Janine turned and looked at him, her eyes wide. "You used meditation on your own?"

He laughed. "What? Are you saying that's not okay? Did I unleash some forces of evil because I didn't have my teacher beside me?"

"No, of course not. You can meditate anytime you

want. I'm just so proud of you!" Without thinking, she reached her arm around and quickly hugged his shoulders before letting go. "Sorry."

He smiled. "I know I might seem like a jerk sometimes, but I don't mind the occasional hug."

"I'm just really impressed at how well you've been doing. I honestly didn't think you would keep at this, but I'm so excited to see that it's making a difference for you."

He turned and looked back at the water, taking a long sip of his coffee. "I didn't think it would work either. But after not seeing my mother for all those years and feeling like an orphan, I was ready to do just about anything to put things back on track. The more I meditate, the more I realize what a jerk I was. I have a lot of apologizing to do."

"I'm sure your mother forgives you."

He paused for a moment, the look on his face changing, like he was keeping something inside. Rather than push, Janine took a sip of her coffee and just waited to see if he wanted to open up about it.

"There is something you don't know."

"What do you mean?"

"There's something I've never told anyone."

"You don't have to tell me anything, Will. But, if you want to, you can trust me."

He sat for a few more moments, taking another sip of coffee and looking at the water. Finally, without looking at her, he spoke. "The real reason I stayed away so long wasn't because I was mad at my mother, although that's how I expressed it. I was mad at myself."

"Mad at yourself? For what?"

"This is hard to say," he said, clearing his throat. "I knew my dad had cancer two months before my mom found out."

Janine was stunned. "How?"

"I overheard him on the phone with his doctor one day. His plan was to never tell any of us and just hopefully pass away in his sleep. I don't think he realized how much the cancer was going to ravage his body."

"What did you do?"

"I sat on the information for a few days and then I finally confronted him about it while Mom was out shopping one day. He told me in no uncertain terms that he didn't want to die like his own father had. Grandpa had gone through all kinds of treatments when he was diagnosed with lung cancer, and the end had not been pretty. He lost his hair and was miserable and my dad just didn't want to go through that."

"How did Dixie finally find out?"

"After a couple of months, my dad started really losing weight. She forced him to go to the doctor, and there she found out the truth. She learned that he had known for a while, but my dad never gave me up. He didn't want my mom to know that I knew so far in advance."

"I don't understand. If you knew your father didn't want treatment, why did you get so mad at your mother?"

"I guess because I wanted somebody to blame. I felt so guilty inside of myself that I couldn't do something to make him change his mind. I kept checking into treatments and telling him about them, but he refused. My mom had always been the stronger one, so I thought she could do something if she just tried hard enough. She was my only hope to change his mind, and when she said she couldn't, I just didn't believe her."

"Oh, wow, I'm so sorry that you have carried that guilt with you all these years. But, it wasn't your fault. And it wasn't Dixie's fault. It wasn't even your father's fault. Bad things just happen, and he had to make the final decision on what was okay for him."

"I'm realizing that more now. Being back here has brought back so many good memories but some bad ones also. Like the day he died. It was the worst day of my life, Janine. To see him lying there in the bed, having lost so much weight. He couldn't communicate because they had to give him so much pain medication. I just remember sitting with him alone toward the end and telling him it was okay to go. That we would be fine, all the while knowing that I was leaving as soon as the funeral was over. I was so angry at him and my mother and even God. I felt like I had no control. I was mad at myself more than anything, but I needed someone to blame, and she became an easy scapegoat."

She wiped away a tear. "I'm curious. Why did you decide to tell me this?"

"I don't know. I guess when you meditate with someone every morning, you start to trust them."

Janine smiled. "You know you have to tell your mom."

Will sighed and fell back onto the mat, staring up at the blue sky. "I know. I just don't know how I'm going to do that. She's going to hate me."

"Look, if there's one thing that I know about Dixie, it's that she is the most forgiving person on the planet. Otherwise, why would she have allowed you back into her life?"

He laughed. "I'm not sure that was a nice thing to say."

Janine laid back on her mat too. "Sometimes, being nice isn't nearly as effective as telling the truth. I don't have kids, but I'm not sure I would've allowed you back into my world after the way you acted. She did. And that tells me she will forgive you for this too."

"I hope you're right. It's forgiving myself I'm having a problem with. My dad would be so mad at me if he knew what I have done. I wasted all those years with my mom, and now she's got this disease that is going to progressively take her away from me."

"You can't think about all of that. One step at a time. Control what you can control, and leave the rest up to God."

He turned and looked at her. "You know, I'm really sorry about what happened to you. I honestly didn't mean to scare you that first day we met here at the beach."

"I know. I won't hold it against you."

"Honestly, it makes me so angry when I think about someone taking advantage of you like that. You're really a nice person, Janine. And, if you ever need to talk, just know that I'm here for you like you've been here for me."

She was stunned by the words he was saying. This didn't seem at all like the same guy who had been so snarky and sarcastic to her when they first met. In just the last couple of weeks, he seemed to have grown so much.

"Thank you. It's nice to have a friend."

"I have a lot of amends I need to make. I know Dawson hates me, my mom doesn't understand why I did what I did and I'm not sure how I feel about your sister."

"My sister is a wonderful person. You'll love her once you get to know her. Say, why don't you come over for dinner tonight and we'll invite Dawson too.

That way we can all chat and get to know each other better."

He sat up, his eyes wide. "I'm not so sure that's a good idea. Dawson wants to strangle me."

"Are you scared?"

" A little," he said with a smile.

CHAPTER 8

*W*illiam sat across the table from his mother, making small talk over lunch. He was trying to do what Janine had suggested by telling her what had really happened when his father died. But, so far, all he had managed to talk about was the weather and how he needed some new shoes because the ones he bought were too tight.

As usual, his mother knew something was up. She kept eyeing him carefully, like she was waiting for the other shoe to drop, so to speak.

"William, it's not that I don't enjoy having lunch with you, but we have had our meal, our dessert and a cup of coffee, and you still look like something's on your mind. What's going on?"

He sucked in a deep breath and slowly blew it out. "Okay, I have something I want to tell you. But

114

please realize that I'm really new to all this meditation stuff, and I'm trying to keep myself calm and go about this in a levelheaded manner..."

Dixie stared at him, her head cocked to the side like a dog who had heard a loud noise. "Goodness, son, what has gotten into you? Why are you so jumpy?"

"I knew about Dad."

"What?"

"I knew about Dad's cancer before you did."

"What are you talking about?"

"I overheard Dad on the phone with his doctor a couple of months before you finally forced him to go see his other doctor. I knew he had cancer. "

Dixie sat there, shocked, staring at him like she didn't understand the words. "How? Why?"

"Look, Mom, I know this is a surprise to you. I tried to get him to go get treatment for all those weeks. He refused. He swore me to secrecy and wouldn't let me tell you that he had cancer. He didn't want to go through what Grandpa went through. So I kept the secret. And then when he started getting really sick and you found out about the cancer, I thought you could do something. I thought you could force his hand, make him go for treatment."

"But you've been mad at me all these years and you knew before I did?"

"It doesn't make any sense, I realize that. I was just so angry. I was angry at him, I was angry that you couldn't do something. But most of all, I was angry at myself for keeping the secret. Maybe if I had told you two months before, you could've done something before it was too far gone. It was my fault!"

To Dixie's surprise, her son's eyes welled with tears. He looked distraught, devastated, and all she wanted to do was hug him.

"William," she said, reaching across the table and holding his hand. "This wasn't your fault. Your father was the most stubborn ox I've ever met in my life! And we all only get one bite at the apple. We all get one life. And your father had the right to decide how he wanted his to go. We fought constantly about his treatment for the first few weeks of his diagnosis. I begged, pleaded, cried, literally got down on my knees one time. I prayed. I called out to God to change his mind. And you know what? He didn't. That's not what Johnny wanted."

"I know that now. It took me coming back here and facing my demons to realize that there was nothing any of us could do. But I feel terrible about how I treated you, how long I let it go on and all the years of your life that I missed."

"We have right now. We can't look at the past, William. We have to move forward from here. I'm so glad you told me the truth because now it makes more sense to me."

"Do you know that I haven't even been dating

much over these last ten years because I didn't want to get serious about somebody and have you miss my wedding?"

She smiled. "Well, I hate that you've been alone, but I sure am glad I didn't miss something like that."

"Me too. I love you, Mom. And I'm so sorry about all of this. I'm learning how to be a different kind of man, how to push all of this darkness out of my mind and heart. I feel different. I'm hopeful again."

"Well, I'll have to thank Janine the next time I see her."

"Yeah, she's a pretty cool woman."

Dixie looked at her son and knew exactly what was going through his mind. He had his eyes set on Janine, and she wasn't sure whether either of them were ready for something serious. But one thing she had learned in all of her years was to keep her big nose out of other people's business.

JULIE STIRRED the big pot of chili as Janine finished mixing the ingredients for corn bread. There was no better combination than chili and cornbread in the cold winter months, although Seagrove wasn't exactly a freezing, snowy metropolis.

"So, tell me again why you are subjecting us to William coming to dinner?" Julie asked.

"He's a nice guy. He's changed a lot. In fact, I

think he had lunch with Dixie today to air out some things. I bet they will get along so much better after that lunch."

Julie stopped stirring and stared at her sister. "Why do I get the feeling you know a lot more than you're letting on?"

"Because I do. But he's my friend, and there's doctor patient confidentiality…"

"You're not a doctor!" Julie said with a laugh.

"I consider myself a doctor of meditation and yoga. In fact, I think I'm going to print up a certificate and hang it on the wall of my imaginary office."

"You're a nut."

"Yes, but I'm your nut!" Janine said, laying her head on her sister's shoulder.

"I'm willing to give William another chance, but only because he's Dixie's son. I'd really like for her to have a relationship with him, and I certainly can't be bad mouthing him."

"Hello?" Dawson called as he walked into the house. He was carrying a covered dish. "Lucy would not let me leave the house without this peach cobbler," he said, handing it to Julie. He leaned down and kissed her on the cheek, something that surprised her.

"Tell her I said thank you. Maybe you can take home a little bit of this chili if we have some left. I remember her saying how she liked it."

"Will do. So, I understand William is coming?" he said, looking Janine's direction.

"Yes, he is. He wants things to get back to normal and I would really appreciate it if you guys would give him a chance. Try to put all of the negative stuff in the back of your mind and just listen to him."

"I'll try. Look, I loved the guy when we were younger. I know the real William is in there somewhere."

"Yes, and my sister has been bringing it out of him by doing morning meditations on the beach."

Dawson turned to look at Janine again. A slight smile on his face. "Oh, don't tell me you're interested in William."

"I never said that. We are friends. We've both gone through some stuff, and I was trying to help him get back with his mother. And guess what, it worked. So there!" she said, sticking out her tongue playfully.

"If you got William on the right path, you're a miracle worker."

There was a knock at the door just then, so Julie walked across the living room to answer it. When she opened it, William was standing there, a slight smile on his face, holding a jug of what appeared to be sweet tea.

"My mom said never to show up at a dinner party without sweet tea ," he said, with a nervous laugh.

"Well, I have to say that is good advice and that

your appearance at my door with an actual smile on your face is quite different than we experienced on Christmas."

He nodded. "I'd like to apologize for that. I was going through a tough time. But, I'd like to get to know you, Julie. My mom thinks very highly of you."

"Well, I think very highly of her. Come on in."

William walked into the house and said hello to everyone. Dawson was still a little standoffish, but he shook his hand anyway.

A few minutes later, Julie was bringing the plates to the table while Janine poured the drinks. They chatted as they waited for the cornbread to finish cooking. William talked about his new job and apartment while Dawson brought him up-to-date on his contracting business. But, everything they talked about was pretty surface level.

Julie couldn't help but notice the awkwardness between Dawson and William. These two childhood friends seemed to be almost distant acquaintances now. She wasn't sure that they would ever be able to get back together the way they were as kids. Dawson held a lot of resentment because he loved Dixie like his own mother.

"This chili is amazing!" William said as he took the first bite.

"Thank you. I'm glad you like it."

"I made the cornbread," Janine felt the need to add.

"I'm sure it will be good." William said.

Julie watched her sister and William carefully. She couldn't quite decide if they were interested in each other or just really good friends, but either way it made her a bit nervous. The last thing she wanted was for her sister to get hurt.

"So, I understand you're partners with my mom now?" William said. Julie had wondered when that was going to come up.

"Yes. She surprised me. I had no idea she was even considering something like that."

She expected him to erupt with anger. She thought he was going to yell at her or say something sarcastic. But then he surprised her.

"I think that's nice. She really loves you, and I know that you love her too. I feel like her business is in good hands if something bad were to happen.

Julie looked at him for a moment. "Thank you. That's really kind of you to say. I was worried you might think I was stepping on some toes by agreeing."

"At first, it did bother me a little. I'll admit that. I mean, I would like for my mother to trust me with something like that, but I know we have some history. The most important thing to me right now is just re-establishing my relationship with her."

"I hope you mean that, man. I really do." Dawson looked at him for a moment and then went back to eating.

"I do. And I'm going to prove it. Being back here has really changed me, and I hope that you and I can spend some time together, Dawson. I've missed having you in my life."

Dawson smiled slightly, nodded his head and went back to eating. It was a step in the right direction, and Julie hoped that all of it would work out one way or another.

JULIE WAS NERVOUS. Even though she was so excited to see Colleen and meet her boyfriend, she had to admit that she was a bit trepidatious. The worst thing she could imagine would be not liking the men that her daughters had chosen as life partners. She wanted a great big happy family with tons of grand-kids one day.

As she fluffed the pillows in the guest room and tightened up the bedding, she was reminded of doing the same thing when her girls were little and she redecorated their room as a surprise one Christmas.

She and Michael had worked so hard to create the perfect princess bedroom complete with canopy twin beds and a beautiful mural on the wall that featured all of their favorite things including a castle, a mermaid and a unicorn. It definitely wasn't Van Gogh, but the girls loved it.

Now her baby girl had grown up to be a beautiful, smart woman. And she had to trust that she made the right decision picking a guy to spend her time with. So, as much as it might be difficult, Julie was determined to like him. Determined to welcome him into her crazy new life.

"I love the linens you chose in here," Janine said, as she walked up behind her.

"Thanks. I got them from that little shop on Elm, the one that Dixie recommended. You don't think they're too dark for the room?"

Janine laughed and hugged her sister from behind. "No, sis. They're perfect. And Colleen is going to be so happy to see you. It's been almost a year since you saw her, hasn't it?"

"Yes. I'm so glad she has the opportunity in California, but I sure wish it was closer to home."

"Me too. I miss both of the girls."

Julie turned around and poked out her lip. "I'm so sorry we had so many years apart. I know how much you love my daughters, and I blocked a lot of the time you could've spent with them. But I'm glad that we have a chance to make things right again."

"It wasn't all your fault. We both had our share in the mess we created. But we're here now, and things are going to be good."

"Yes, they are. My baby is coming to visit, and I'm going to soak up every ounce of time I have with her!"

"When will she be here?"

"Tomorrow evening. I'm cooking a nice, big roast and vegetables to welcome them here."

"Nice! So, what's your plan for today? I mean besides constantly fluffing these same pillows?" Janine asked, taking the pillow from her hand.

Julie laughed. "Nervous habit. Actually, today Dawson is taking me to lunch at some new seafood place in town."

"Hmmm... That sounds awfully romantic."

"Oh please, Miss Morning Meditations with a handsome stranger."

"Is he handsome? I hadn't noticed." Janine dropped the pillow and walked out of the room, Julie hot on her heels.

"You know he's a good looking guy. I've seen how you look at him," Julie said as she followed her into the living room.

"He's my friend."

"And Dawson is my friend."

"Do you often kiss your friends?" Janine asked, her hand on her hip.

"Only if they're really nice to me," Julie retorted with a laugh as she slapped her sister on the arm and walked to the kitchen.

~

JULIE SQUEALED like a kid at Christmas when she opened her front door and saw her daughter standing there. Even though she knew Colleen was coming, she was super excited to see her in the flesh after almost a year apart. She grabbed her daughter and pulled her into a hug, not wanting to let her go.

"I cannot believe you're here!" she said, pressing her lips to her daughter's cheek before finally pulling back. Janine, standing behind her, slipped in and hugged Colleen tightly.

"I'm so glad to see both of you!" Colleen said, her eyes watering.

Julie couldn't help but notice that Colleen seemed to be alone. "Where is Peter?"

"Oh, I asked him to let me come alone tonight, just to spend some time with you two. He's going to come in the morning so we can all have breakfast together."

"But I thought you two were staying here while you visited?"

"We are. But he decided to get a room for the night on the mainland. He's working on a big contract, and I wanted some girl time."

Janine picked up Colleen's suitcase and walked into the living room. Julie ushered her daughter inside and shut the door. It was getting cold outside, even by Seagrove standards. She had seen frost that morning on the cordgrass in the marsh behind the house.

"This is the most adorable little island I have ever seen!" Colleen said with a smile. "And the sunset coming in was stunning."

"Yes, it's like a little slice of heaven on earth."

"Mom, this house is adorable too. You guys have done such a great job decorating it!"

"I hope you like the guest room. I bought brand new linens for you."

Colleen hugged her mom again. "You didn't have to do that, Mom."

"I wanted it to be perfect!"

"It's such a relief to see both of you. Aunt Janine, it's been so long!"

Janine stepped forward and hugged her niece again, causing Julie to feel so guilty about the years that she kept them apart. Colleen had adored her aunt Janine as a child, and even though she knew over the years they had still spoken by phone and the occasional email, she had been so adamant that they not see each other. Looking back, she realized now that Janine was just being herself and giving advice to her daughters that she would give to her own child if she had one. But, for some reason, it had felt so threatening to Julie at the time.

"How about some pot roast? I made a full meal with all your favorites!"

Colleen smiled sadly. "I'm sorry, Mom. I ate on the plane, and I'm still really full. But I'd love a cup of coffee if you have one."

Julie felt a little deflated. Pot roast had always been Colleen's favorite meal that she made. Although she wasn't the world's best cook, her kids had appreciated some of the dishes she commonly prepared.

"Sure. Janine, would you mind putting on a pot?"

"Sure."

"Come on over here and sit down. I want to hear all about your trip and your job and the new love in your life."

Colleen followed her over to the sofa and sat down close to her mother. They held each other's hands like if they didn't, they might be separated. Colleen had always been the one that looked most like her mother. She had long blonde hair, perfectly styled, and porcelain skin. She was tall, thin and athletic. Very different from her sister, Meg, who was petite and dark-haired, much more like Michael.

"The trip was good. A little bit of turbulence, but pretty much a nonevent. Peter has traveled all over the world, so he's used to that sort of thing. He kept me calm."

"Oh, so Peter is a world traveler? Was his father in the military or something?"

Colleen giggled. "No. Peter is from a very wealthy family. They own a large media conglomerate, and Peter does the legal work for them. He's been to so many countries, it's hard to keep up."

"Wow! Got you a rich one!" Janine called from the

kitchen.

"Yes, but that really doesn't matter to me. I mean, I want a successful man, obviously. But the amount of money in his bank account really doesn't affect me. I want to make my own money. We keep everything separate."

Julie nodded and squeezed her daughter's hand. "That's very smart. You can't rely on a man for..." She hung her head. "I'm sorry. I shouldn't say something like that."

Colleen looked at her mother. "Mom, it's okay. We all know what Dad did. And you're right, you shouldn't rely on a man."

"Let's not talk about your father. That's old news for me, and I don't want to beat a dead horse."

Colleen looked a little funny, but Janine interrupted their conversation by handing her a cup of coffee."

"So, where is this Dawson fellow I kept hearing you talk about?"

"My friend, Dawson, is at his house tonight, I would assume."

"A little birdie told me that he kissed you on New Year's Eve," Colleen said, taking a sip of her coffee and batting her eyelashes.

"Janine! I can't trust you with anything!" Julie said, smacking her sister on the side as she stood next to them. "Sorry! I just thought it was really cute."

"Well, it doesn't matter. Nothing serious is going on. We are taking it very slow. He lost his wife and baby several years ago, and I think Dawson still has some healing to do from that."

Colleen looked shocked. "That's terrible!"

"So, tell me more about this Peter. He comes from a rich family and he does legal work. But what's he like?"

Colleen grinned from ear to ear. "He's super handsome. He's tall, dark and handsome, like some kind of romantic hero in a book. Very well read. Loves playing polo and golf."

"Polo? I don't think I've ever known anyone who actually played polo."

"Well, Mom, you have to get out of the South."

Julie was bothered by that comment. She had never raised her daughters to judge any type or group of people. And she certainly didn't like any stereotypical comments about different parts of the country.

"Sweetie, I'm sure there are people in the South who play polo. I just haven't met any of them."

"Of course. I didn't mean anything by that."

"Good. Why don't you let me show you your room, and you can go ahead and start unpacking some of your things."

"Sounds good. I'll follow you," Colleen said.

The women stayed up talking for several hours, drinking pot after pot of coffee. But the extra caffeine did nothing to keep Colleen awake. She was exhausted from a long day of traveling and went to bed around ten o'clock. Janine and Julie took the time to sit out on the back deck and wind down.

"Do you get the feeling being out in California has changed Colleen a bit?" Janine asked.

"Maybe. I don't like the way she was talking about the South. We're pretty proud of our South-ernness."

"Well, most of it," Janine joked. "We have our share of skeletons in the closet."

"True. Anyway, I just hope I like this guy."

"I think you're worrying too much. Colleen has a good head on her shoulders. You raised her well."

"Thanks. Your yoga classes start in the morning, don't they?"

"They do! I'm so excited and scared at the same time. Plus, these morning frosts lately might keep people from coming out."

"Now, I think you're worrying too much!" Julie chided.

They sat quietly for a few minutes. "You know, I think it's amazing where we are now."

"You mean on the island?"

"Well, yes, that too. But I mean our relationship. I so missed having a sister," Janine said, reaching over and touching Julie's arm.

"Me too."

CHAPTER 9

*C*olleen finished getting ready while Julie started preparing breakfast. Janine had left early to teach her class, and Julie hoped she would have a good turnout. It wasn't so cold that morning, so she crossed her fingers that Janine's new venture would pay off.

As she stirred the scrambled eggs, she thought about how this was a watershed moment. She was about to meet the man her daughter was serious about, and something about that felt so monumental. She pulled the biscuits out of the oven and set the strawberry preserves that Lucy had made on the counter next to the butter. Hopefully this guy liked a good Southern breakfast.

The bacon was sitting on two paper towels as the oil drained away, and the cheese grits were already cooling in a bowl. Now, all that was left was to set out the orange juice and coffee. She scurried around like a crazy person, putting the finishing touches on the table. When she heard a knock at the door, she ran to open it, expecting to see Peter.

"Welcome to my…" she said, as she opened the door. She stopped short when she found herself staring into the eyes of her ex husband instead of Colleen's boyfriend. "Michael?"

"Hello, Julie." He was alone, thank goodness, and was using a cane. She hadn't asked for details about his recovery from Colleen, not wanting to care about how he was doing. It was hard after all those years of marriage, all of those good memories. Amazing how someone can make choices that wipe all of that away and leave a person with so much anger and hate.

She stepped out onto the porch, pushing him away from the door with her momentum, and closed the door behind her. "Michael, you're not welcome here. How did you even know where I live?"

"Legal documents, Julie. My attorney has sent a lot of mail here in the last few months."

She nodded. "Right. Well, why are you here?"

Colleen stepped out from the house. "Dad?" She walked over and hugged him tightly. Michael hugged her with one arm, his other hand tightly grasping his cane.

"Pumpkin, I'm so glad to see you," he said, his

eyes welling with tears. Julie hadn't seen that side of him in a long time.

Colleen looked at her mother and then back at her father. "I thought we were meeting up later tonight, Dad?"

"I couldn't wait to see my baby girl. I'm sorry."

"You shouldn't have come here," Colleen said. "I'm sorry, Mom."

In that moment, Julie felt bad for her daughter. She'd spent her whole life with seemingly happy parents, and now they wouldn't even look at each other. How was this going to play out in years to come? At weddings? The birth of grandchildren? Even if Michael was a louse, Julie decided she didn't have to be.

"Come inside, Michael. I'm sure you're tired of standing up," she said, aware that he was still deep in rehabilitation for all of his injuries.

He stared at her for a long moment. "Really?" Colleen froze in place, obviously unsure of what was happening.

"Of course. We believe in Southern hospitality around here."

She opened the door and stood back, allowing Colleen and Michael to walk inside. She pointed to the living room, and they all sat down.

"Look, I realize I probably shouldn't have come here, Julie. I'm sorry that I didn't give you any warning, but I wanted to surprise our daughter."

"And I'm taking the high road for her."

"I appreciate that," he said, before turning his attention back to Colleen. "So, where's the new guy?"

"He's on his way," Colleen said, looking down at her phone. "I can't wait for ya'll to meet him."

"He better be a good man if he's dating my daughter," Michael said.

"Yes, we wouldn't want her to get with the wrong man," Julie said under her breath. Michael looked at her, knowing exactly what she meant.

"I hate to leave you two alone, but I need to finish my makeup. Is that okay?" Colleen asked, looking more at her mother than her father.

Julie smiled. "Of course, honey."

She walked down the hallway, leaving Julie and Michael alone in the living room. Awkward silence permeated the room.

"Nice place," Michael finally said, although she doubted that he meant it. Michael hated the ocean, and small houses weren't his thing either. He probably thought she was destitute.

"Thanks. So, where's Victoria?"

He cleared his throat. "She and Charlie are back at the hotel. I didn't think it was appropriate to bring them here."

"Well, at least you knew that much."

Michael sighed. "Look, I apologized for coming here, Jules... I mean, Julie. It's just that knowing

Colleen was so close, well, I couldn't stay away. The accident really made me reassess my life, and my girls are so important to me."

"I get that, Michael. I just don't know how to navigate this new relationship we have. We're going to be stuck together for the rest of our lives, and it's still hard for me."

"I'm sorry. I really am. When you came to take care of me, I was in a bad place. They had me so doped up, I didn't know whether I was coming or going. I said and did things I wouldn't normally say or do. I feel awful about how I treated you when you took care of me. You didn't have to do what you did, and I want you to know I appreciate it."

"Michael, I don't get one thing. Victoria left you when you were at your lowest, and yet you went back to her. Why? I mean, I know it's not my problem or my business now, but I am curious."

He looked at her and shrugged his shoulders. "I don't know, honestly. I just know she's not like you. She's not a nurturer. She's good with Charlie, of course, but she just can't always handle tough stuff."

"And that's the kind of woman you want to hitch your wagon to for life?"

"I love her."

Julie was taken aback to hear him say it to her face for some reason. Before she could respond, Colleen came back out into the living room.

"He's here!" she said as she ran to the front door

and swung it open. Peter was coming up the walk-way, and she ran out to greet him, planting a big kiss on him before she pulled him into the house.

He wasn't exactly what Julie expected. He had striking, almost harsh features with a square jawline and thick, almost intimidating eyebrows. He was tall, as Colleen had said, but thin. While everyone else was wearing casual clothing, he was dressed in a dress shirt, slacks and had a tie on, not at all what most people wore on the island.

"Mom, Dad, this is Peter Wellman," Colleen said, smiling broadly as Peter shook her father's hand. He nodded at Julie, and although she normally hugged everyone she met, he stepped back. She could tell he wasn't a hugger, for sure.

"Nice to meet you both," Peter said, barely a hint of a smile on his face.

"We've heard good things about you," Julie said. Something about him made her uneasy, but she tried to push the feeling away. "I hope you're hungry."

"Famished," he said.

"Why don't we go sit at the table and get to know each other?" She took in a deep breath and summoned her inner strength. "Michael, would you like to join us?"

He looked at her, a bit of shock on his face. "Um, sure. Thank you."

They sat down, and Julie brought the food to the table, along with a big bowl of cut up fruit. Colleen piled fruit on her plate as Peter did the same. Julie waited for them to take some of the other food, but neither did.

"Peter, would you like some eggs? Or bacon?"

He scrunched his face a bit. "No thank you. I'm vegan. Colleen is too. I'm surprised you didn't warn your mother, babe."

Colleen smiled. "I'm sorry, Mom. I forgot to tell you. But, this fruit is great."

Julie froze in her seat. "So, that's why you didn't want the roast last night?"

"Yes. I'm sorry. But, don't worry, we'll do a little grocery shopping so you won't have to worry about cooking for us."

"You made the roast?" Michael whispered to her.

"Yes. Why?"

"I just always loved your roast," he said, surprising her. It was moments like that that made her long for the early days of their marriage, the times when he only had eyes for her. Where had it all gone wrong? "So, Peter, Colleen tells me your family owns a media company?"

"Yes. We own radio and TV stations, mostly. A couple of newspapers. We're currently starting a new network news channel too, although that will be years in the making."

"Impressive," Michael said.

Colleen looked at Peter and smiled. "We have something to tell you guys."

Julie and Michael looked at each other and then back at Colleen. "Okay…"

"We're engaged! I didn't want to tell you until we could see you in person!"

Julie felt her lungs empty, and then she couldn't seem to suck in a deep enough breath to respond. She wanted to be happy, but her daughter was still so young, still so much of herself to find before getting married. All sorts of things flashed through her mind when she heard the news. She saw her baby in her arms, her first steps, the first time she rode a bike.

And then she thought about Peter. He seemed… detached. He wasn't really even smiling. What did he want with her daughter? What kind of husband would he be?

"Mom? Did you hear me?"

Michael stared at her, a look of warning on his face. "Julie?"

"Oh, wow, yes. How exciting! I'm so happy for you both!" She managed to fake it as she stood up and hugged her daughter tightly. This time, Peter allowed her to hug him, but it was like embracing a dog that really wanted to just bite you in the face.

"I have to say, I'm a little disappointed," Michael suddenly said.

"Disappointed? Why, Dad?"

"I guess as your father, I just expected Peter here

would've asked your parents for your hand in marriage before proposing."

Julie was stunned, yet sort of impressed, that Michael had spoken up.

"Pardon me for saying so, sir, but isn't that an antiquated, patriarchal way to do things?" Peter said, those intimidating eyebrows practically jumping across the table.

"Excuse me?"

"Okay, why don't we focus on the positive part of this, guys? I'm getting married!" Colleen said, trying to keep the two men from coming to blows.

"You'll be a beautiful bride, sweetie," Julie said. "But, isn't this kind of sudden? I mean, you've only known each other a few months, right? What's the hurry?"

Colleen stared at her mother. "Jeez, this was supposed to be good, exciting news. I have to say I'm underwhelmed at the response we've gotten. I think I need some air. Come on, Peter," she said, standing up and putting her napkin on the table.

"Colleen, come on… we're just surprised…" Julie said as they walked out the front door. "Well, we could've handled that better, I guess," she said.

"Maybe," Michael said, biting into a piece of bacon. "I don't like this guy."

Finally, something they could agree on. He didn't seem at all suited to their daughter, but maybe she had changed since living in California for the last year.

"We don't get to make that choice for her, though. Aren't we running the risk of pushing her away if we keep saying things?"

"Julie, he's the wrong guy. We have to say something."

She smiled sadly. "This feels so familiar."

"What does?"

"Eating brunch with you, talking about our kids. Trying to have a united front."

He nodded. "Yeah, I know what you mean."

"I smell bacon!" Julie turned to see Dawson walking through her back door, as he often did in the mornings. "Oh, sorry. I seem to have interrupted... sorry." He turned and walked back toward the deck.

"No, please come in, Dawson."

He stopped and stood there, unsure of what he'd walked into, obviously.

"This is Michael, my ex husband."

Michael glared at Dawson, and he did the same. It was like two raging bulls staring at each other. The only thing missing was the blowing of air out of their snouts and kicking up dirt.

"Hello," Dawson finally said, not making his normal move of shaking hands.

"Hey." Michael stood up, pressing his hand against his cane.

"I didn't know you were entertaining this morning, Julie."

"Colleen and her... fiance... are here for brunch. They just stepped out to get some air."

"Her fiancé?"

"Yeah. We just got blindsided. I didn't know Michael was coming. That part was a surprise."

"Oh. Well, I'll let ya'll get back to it." Dawson turned again and she followed him out onto the deck, shutting the door behind them.

"Hey," she said, staring up at him. "I had no idea he was coming. Neither did Colleen. They were supposed to meet up tonight. His girlfriend and kid are at a hotel on the mainland."

"Sorry. I was just thrown when I saw you in there with a guy, and then when you said who it was... well, I'm going to be honest... I wanted to slug him one good time. Or maybe a few times. I was going to wing it."

Julie giggled. "Thanks, but I'm okay."

"If you need me, you know how to reach me. I've got plenty of pent up anger, and I'd love to unleash it on that guy."

"It's actually been pleasant so far, surprisingly. Maybe we're past being angry at each other, and we can just be co-parents."

"Good for you."

"I'll see you later, okay?" she said. He bent down

and kissed her cheek in full view of Michael through the window.

"I'm a text away."

She waved goodbye and walked back inside. Michael looked down at his food and took a bite as she sat back down.

"I thought they'd be back by now."

"You know Colleen. She needs to cool off. I'm sure they'll be back soon. So, is that your new boyfriend?"

"He's my very good friend, Dawson."

"Ah, so that's the infamous Dawson. The one you talked to on the phone that day when you were in Boston."

"Yes."

"Is it serious?"

She stood up and put her plate in the kitchen, her appetite gone. "Michael, I'm not discussing this with you."

He stood up and followed her. "I just care about you, Julie."

"Do you? Really? Because your actions these last few months certainly didn't indicate that. Look, we're co-parents. That's it. We will never be anything else. Not in a relationship. Not buddies. Not friends. Just co-parents."

"I hope he's a decent guy. That's all."

Julie turned and looked at him. "He's an amazing

man, Michael." She wanted to say so much more, but she refrained. Today had been hard enough.

The front door opened, and Colleen walked back inside alone. Through the window, she could see Peter pulling out of the driveway.

"He's leaving?" Michael said.

"What else is he supposed to do? Stay here with my parents who obviously don't like him?" Julie could tell Colleen had been crying. She walked over and took her hand.

"We just don't know him yet, honey."

"Which is why he came here, to get to know you. But you made him feel unwelcome. He's a good person, and he loves me."

"I'm sorry he didn't feel welcome, but you have to understand we're a little shellshocked, Colleen. I mean, you've only been dating a few months and now you're marrying him?"

She stood taller and pushed her shoulders back, her normal stance when she was about to assert herself. Julie imagined that was how she'd look in court one day when she was prosecuting criminals. Colleen had always been tough as nails.

"You don't have to love him or even like him. But, if you love me, you have to welcome him too because he's going to be my husband whether you like it or not. Now, I'm going to pack my things and call an Uber to take me to the hotel. I sent him away because he had a business call, but he's expecting me soon."

"Sweetie, please stay. Have Peter come back, and let's talk this out."

"No, Mom. I don't think that's a good idea. You know, I was so excited about coming here. I thought this news would be a new beginning for our family, a way to heal some of what happened this year. I guess not."

Without another word, she walked down the hallway and quietly closed the door to the guest room, leaving Julie and Michael to stare at each other and wonder what to do next.

CHAPTER 10

"*Y*ikes. That sounds horrible," William said, as Janine relayed what had happened with Julie and her daughter.

"Yeah, it was quite a scene, from what I understand. I just feel so bad for my sister. I tried to call Colleen this morning, but she didn't answer."

William rolled up his mat and handed it to Janine. "Family stuff is hard sometimes."

"Yeah, it definitely is."

"So, how did your first class go yesterday?"

Janine smiled sadly. "Not great. Only had three people, even though at least ten had signed up. Can't make ends meet with three people."

"Hey, you're just starting out. What kind of marketing did you do?"

"I put it on Dixie's bulletin board."

He stared at her. "That's it?"

"Pretty much."

William laughed. "You have to do more marketing than that, Janine."

"I'm not exactly a marketing expert, Will," she said, rolling up her own mat.

He grinned. "Well, I am. Come on, we have some work to do."

JULIE HAD BEEN THRILLED when Colleen finally texted her at lunch time. She asked her to meet in town at a wedding dress shop. Not wanting to rock the boat, Julie decided to just go with the flow and do the best she could to respect her daughter's decisions and support her.

"Hey, Mom," Colleen said as her mother met her on the sidewalk in front of the store.

"Hey, sweetie. Look, I just wanna say I'm sorry about yesterday..."

"Let's just not talk about it. I want to enjoy the time that I'm here with you."

Julie smiled. "Okay. I'm looking forward to seeing you try on some dresses."

"So are we," Michael said, as he came around the corner of the building. He wasn't alone. Victoria stood there, holding their son, looking quite uncomfortable.

"Hello, Julie," she said softly.

146

"Why is she here?" Julie asked, not making eye contact with her, but instead glaring at Michael.

"She's part of our family now."

"She's not part of my family," Julie said.

Colleen looked at her father. "Did you really think this was the best idea, Dad?"

"I can't leave her in the hotel the entire time."

"If you want me to go, I will do that." Victoria turned and started walking down the sidewalk.

"No, honey, come back." Michael walked to her and pulled her back toward the store. "This woman is going to be my wife soon, and she's going to be involved in all of these things. We have to find some way of making this work."

"Fine. Today is about Colleen, so let's just try to get along." Julie turned and looked at her daughter. "Are you ready?"

Colleen smiled and nodded her head. "Yes, I am. I've looked at a few dresses in California, but I thought it was worth a shot to look here since I'm in town."

They walked into the store and were greeted by a super sweet sales lady named Lita. Before long, she was pulling all different kinds of dresses that matched the styles that Colleen was interested in.

The three of them sat down and waited for Colleen to try on the first dress. Michael held his son, and Julie couldn't help but look at them. She remembered those days of watching him take care of their daughters when they were around the same age. He had been a good dad, and that hadn't changed. And for a long time, he had been a phenomenal husband too. It was so hard to split those times up in her mind. She had fond memories but now they were marred by his infidelity. Having to sit there and see him with his mistress and baby was almost more than she could take. But, today was for her daughter, and she would do anything for her kids.

"This is a lovely area, Julie," Victoria finally said. "Very different from Boston."

"I didn't live in Boston."

"I know. I just mean… Never mind."

"Julie lives on a little island across the bridge. You'd love it, honey," he said to Victoria. Again, Julie was thrown for a loop hearing him call someone else honey. That had always been his pet name for her. Although she had no interest in rekindling their relationship, it still felt very strange to hear him use that word and direct it at a different woman.

"I love the ocean. We're thinking about getting a beach house once Charlie gets a little older. Maybe somewhere around here?"

"What do you mean around here? Why wouldn't you get something closer to Boston?" Julie said, getting an uneasy feeling in the pit of her stomach.

"We're just thinking ahead. It gets cold and, since

my accident, the frigid weather is hard for me. We might move down south."

Julie felt like she was swallowing her tongue. "But not here?"

"We haven't made any decisions yet."

"Michael, there's an entire eastern coast. Feel free to move just about anywhere else." She found herself glaring at him again, giving him that look she had always given as a warning shot. The last thing she wanted was for him to come invade her new space.

Thankfully, Colleen came out of the dressing room, wearing a beautiful white gown with a long train. Julie's eyes immediately filled with tears as she held her hands in the prayer position in front of her mouth. "Oh, Colleen, you look so beautiful! I can't believe you're going to be a bride!"

"What do you think?"

"It's a beautiful dress. You look like a princess."

"It is stunning, Colleen." Victoria said. Even Colleen looked blankly in her direction, proving there was definitely no love lost between them.

"I like it, but honestly I'm looking for something a little more simple. Maybe that sleeveless gown with the beads around the neckline?" she said to Lita. She nodded her head.

"I think you're right! Let me get that. Come with me," she said as Colleen followed her back to the dressing room.

"Well, I can't believe our daughter is all grown up," Michael said.

"I know. It seems like just yesterday she was taking her first steps."

"Or being in her first ballet recital," Michael said, reminiscing.

"Do you remember when she fell off her bike on that hiking trail?" Julie said. "I thought her poor little knee would never stop bleeding."

"I'm so worried about when Charlie starts riding a bike. I'm sure that I'm going to follow him around with a box of bandages, just in case," Victoria said.

Julie leaned around Michael and looked at her. "What?"

"Oh, I was just saying that we mothers can be overprotective."

"Please don't lump me in with you. I don't think we are at all the same kind of mother."

"Now, Julie, that was uncalled for. Victoria is a wonderful mother."

"Michael, it's okay. I know she still has hard feelings toward me."

"Hard feelings? You mean because you cheated with my husband and got pregnant? Is that what you mean? Because I have no hard feelings about that. I quite enjoyed being abandoned by Michael while he shacked up with you."

"Julie!" Michael said. "Hold your voice down. This is not the time."

"You're right. It's not worth it. I'm not going to let you or that woman ruin this moment."

Colleen walked back out, this time wearing a simpler white gown with a beaded neckline and shorter train. She had her hair pulled up and looked so regal.

"Oh, Colleen, I honestly think that's the one!" Julie said, a stray tear falling down her cheek.

"I do too!"

The doorbell chimed behind them, and Julie turned to see Peter walking in. He walked over and pecked Colleen on the lips.

"Oh no! The groom isn't supposed to see the bride in her gown before the wedding. It's bad luck!" Julie said.

"No offense, but we really don't buy into the idea of traditional wedding superstitions," he said. Colleen smiled slightly.

"Still, honey, I asked you not to come here. I wanted my gown to be a surprise."

"I think I should have some say so in this, Colleen. It is my wedding too. I'm sure you'll help pick my tux, right?"

"I suppose so," she said, obviously deflated. "So, what do you think of this one, hon?"

He barely looked up from texting on his phone. "It's nice. A bit plain, don't you think? I mean, we are having the wedding at the country club, and I think the dress needs to match the venue, right?"

"I hadn't thought about that. You're probably right. Maybe I should try on a few more," she said, looking at Lita, who also looked shellshocked by Peter's response. "Do you have some that are a bit more elegant?"

"Um… Of course," Lita stammered. "Let me help you get out of this one."

Colleen followed her back to the dressing rooms as Julie struggled not to lose her cool. Being stuck in a room with Peter, Michael and Victoria made her want to run out into traffic, what little there was.

"I need a little air," she said standing up and walking outside. The dress shop was just a block from Down Yonder. She saw Dixie locking up for lunch and waved at her.

"Hey, lady! What are you doing at the wedding dress store? Oh my, did Dawson propose?" Dixie said, clapping her hands.

"No, of course not! My daughter, Colleen, is engaged."

"Really? You never mentioned it."

Julie leaned in and whispered. "It was a shock. In a nutshell, her fiancé seems to be a jerk, and my ex husband and his mistress are also in there. Which is why I'm out here."

Dixie squinted her eyes toward the shop, a look of anger on her face. "You mean the scoundrel's in there?"

"Yep."

"Pardon me, sweetie. This I've gotta see," she said, walking past Julie and into the dress shop before Julie could stop her.

"Everyone, this is my good friend and business partner, Dixie Campbell. Dixie, this is my ex husband, Michael, and Colleen's fiancee, Peter."

Dixie leaned over to shake Peter's hand and then turned her attention to Michael. "Well, well, well, you're the infamous Michael, huh?"

Michael leaned back a bit. "I am…"

"I've heard a lot about you, sir."

"None of it good, I'm sure." He looked at Julie, almost like he was hoping she'd help him, but she decided to let him twist in the wind a bit.

"Not a bit."

Colleen came back out, this time in a fancier dress. She didn't look nearly as excited, which made Julie so sad. A woman should love her wedding dress.

"That's lovely, Colleen," Julie said. It was a nice dress, but not at all her daughter's style.

"Much better," Peter said.

"Colleen, this is my friend, Dixie. She owns the bookstore that we're partners in now."

"Oh, yes, I've heard so much about you, Dixie," Colleen said with a smile. "My mother talks very highly of you."

"You're a beauty, darlin'. Your momma sure does love you."

Colleen smiled. "I love her too."

"Pardon me for saying so, but should the groom be seeing the bride in her dress?"

Julie cleared her throat. "Well, um, they aren't following the traditional wedding stuff."

"Good Lord! That's crazy talk, hon! All that stuff makes a wedding fun. I remember the first time Johnny, my late husband, saw me in my dress. His eyes filled up with tears, and that man never cried. I'll never forget the look on his face."

Colleen looked upset. "Yeah, I've always seen that in the movies."

"Movies are fiction, my love. We live in reality," Peter said, still looking down at his phone.

"Right." Colleen said. "I'm going to go change."

She went back to the dressing room as Dixie sat down right next to Michael. "So, you must be the mistress, huh?" she said to Victoria as she leaned across Michael.

"I… um…"

"That wasn't nice. She's my fiancee."

"Uh huh. That's not what we would've called her back in my day. But, you know what, I don't have a problem with you, dear. You didn't have wedding vows, but this fella sure did."

"I don't see where any of this is your business," Michael said, angrily. "Julie, can you please call her off?"

Julie shrugged her shoulders. "Dixie does what she wants."

Dixie laughed loudly. "You're a bit of a whiner, Michael." She stood up and walked toward the door. "Nice to meet you all," she said, winking at Julie as she left the store.

"Nice friend you have there," Michael said, rolling his eyes.

"Yeah, she's pretty amazing."

JULIE PICKED AT HER FOOD. She had been hungry when she showed up to meet Dawson for lunch, but her mind was wandering. Colleen was leaving in a couple of days, and she hated the thought of her going back to California with a man who obviously didn't love her.

If he loved her, he would care what she thought. He would care what dress she wanted and what traditions she wanted to uphold. Julie, being in her forties, had the benefit of seeing what Colleen's future was going to be like if she stayed with a man who didn't care about her input.

"Are you okay? You haven't touched your meal."

"I'm sorry. I'm just lost in thought. I'm so worried about my daughter."

Dawson reached across the table and squeezed her hand. "Do you wanna talk about it?"

"I don't even know if it will help. I'm just so concerned that she's chosen the wrong man, and it could destroy her life."

"I haven't met the guy, but are you sure that maybe you're not comparing her to you?"

She looked at him, confused. "What do you mean?"

"Well, I mean you chose a guy that you thought was the right guy and then he ended up derailing your life. Is that what you're worried about?"

She shook her head. "No. When Michael and I first got married, and really for the first 15 years of our marriage, he was a wonderful father and husband. But this guy, he's not equipped for either of those things. It's like he's not even connected to this whole process. He's always on his phone, he doesn't appreciate any of our traditions or values. I just don't understand what she sees in him."

"You just have to be careful, Julie. You don't want to push your daughter away."

"That's what I'm worried about. I want to be honest with her. I want to warn her. But, at the same time, I'm well aware of what I would've said to my mom at that age. You just think you know everything. You're running on hormones and emotions, but that will only last so long. Real love stands the test of time."

Dawson smiled. "You're absolutely right. You're a good mom, Julie."

"Well, thank you, but I don't feel like such a good mom right now. I'm going to talk to my daughter, but that means risking our relationship in the process."

"I never got the chance to be a parent, but I know it has to be hard. I don't think you'll ever stop parenting your kids."

She nodded. "Thanks for being here for me. I know it must've been jarring to walk into my house and see my ex-husband sitting there."

He looked down at his food and finally back up at her. "To be honest, I thought maybe something was going on."

"Like what?"

"Like maybe you guys were trying to rekindle something. You looked comfortable and so did he."

She smiled. "Dawson, there is absolutely nothing going on between me and Michael. I was trying to make the best of a bad situation ."

"I know that now. I got a little… jealous."

She stared at him. "Jealous? Of Michael? Have you even looked in the mirror?"

He laughed. "Well, aside from my ravishing good looks, I know he has a long history with you. It would be very easy for you to fall back into that pattern. I know you have conflicting feelings for him."

"Not feelings for him, really. I have memories. Memories of us being newly married. Memories of

157

us being parents together. Memories of Thanksgiving dinners and Christmases and birthdays and skinned knees and fights over where to eat dinner. I have lots of memories. But I also remember the betrayal. The words that were said. And, of course the fact that he got another woman pregnant and left me to fend for myself. All of the memories in the world could never make me want to go back with him."

"Good to know."

"You know, you can have years and years of good times together and then it can unravel in a second. It just has felt so conflicting to me lately that all of those memories don't mean anything anymore. They are just things I remember, but what he did wiped the good feelings away that are associated with a lot of those memories. I guess I grieve those good feelings I lost."

"I'm sorry that I thought something might be going on."

"No, I understand. And I know that you're not ready for anything serious yet, and maybe you never will be. But just know that I've worked through what I was feeling. When I look at Michael, I feel nothing but pity. Because I know what he lost. Not me, but the life that he had with me. The place he had in our family."

"I've been seeing someone."

"What?" she said, her heart starting to pound.

How could she have picked yet another man who wasn't loyal. She was going to look into becoming a nun. She wasn't Catholic, but maybe they could make an exception.

"No, I didn't mean it that way. I mean I've been seeing a counselor for the last few days."

She put her hand to her chest, letting out the breath she had been holding. "You scared me."

"Good. That means you care," he said with a laugh.

"So now that my heart isn't fibrillating anymore, you were saying?"

"I went to a grief support group on Tuesday. And then I saw the counselor from there a couple of times. Talking through what I have been feeling has been really helpful. I'm going to keep going, keep working through the grief I never acknowledged. But I want you to know that I'm interested in a serious relationship with you, Julie. I hope you can just be patient a little while longer."

She smiled and reached across the table, taking his hands. "Dawson Lancaster, if there's one thing I know for sure, it's that you are most certainly worth waiting for."

CHAPTER 11

*J*ulie walked down the sidewalk with her daughter, trying to take in every moment. She had missed her so much over the last year, and she was finding it very hard to grasp the idea that she was leaving the next day to go back to California.

Her wedding was set for the upcoming summer, and Julie was already trying to plan time off from the bookstore to fly out to California. Inside, her stomach was twisting up in knots because she knew she needed to say some things to Colleen before she left.

"Oh my goodness, look at those adorable Christmas decorations on clearance," Colleen said, pointing through the window of one of the numerous shops lining the square.

"And what a great deal," Julie commented, trying

to figure out exactly how she was going to broach the subject of Peter with her daughter.

"You know, I can't wait to have my own house one day. I'll get to decorate it just how I want. There are so many things you did with us around the holidays as kids that I want to carry on with my own children."

"Are you and Peter thinking of starting a family soon? I mean, you're still pretty young."

"Peter really wants me to leave the law firm and come work for his family. Since he's a few years older than me, he really wants to start a family sooner rather than later."

"But what do you want?"

She looked at her mother and smiled slightly. "I'm okay with that."

"Colleen, you're not giving up your dreams, are you?"

They stopped and sat down under a tree on a bench. Julie always loved coming here on her breaks from the bookstore so that she could people watch.

"Why do you think I'm giving up my dreams?"

"I'm just asking. I want to make sure that you're going to get to live out all of your goals. Ever since you were a kid, you wanted to be a prosecutor. But if you go to work for his family, I assume you'll just be doing business law. I don't think that was ever your dream."

Colleen paused for a moment as she watched

people walk by. "I mean, yes, I've always wanted to be a prosecutor. But I'm not sure it would lend itself well to family life."

"I'm sure a lot of prosecutors have families, honey."

"Mom, it kind of feels like you're trying to make me second-guess my engagement. I hope that's not what you're doing."

"Honey, I just want the best for you. And for the first time in a long time, your father and I are both concerned about the same thing."

"Great. It's so nice to know that your parents are talking about you behind your back," she said dryly.

"You're our daughter. We are always going to talk about our kids. That's what parents do."

"You haven't liked Peter since the moment you met him."

"Well, to be honest, I don't think he made all that great of a first impression."

Now things were getting a little more heated than Julie had anticipated. She didn't want to send her daughter all the way back across the country mad at her, but she also wanted to be honest. Parents had to ride that fine line of not telling their kids what to do and letting them live their own lives and telling them when they were about to make a huge mistake.

To her, it was like warning her daughter that there was a big gap in the road ahead, and that her car was going to fly off of it. Sure, she could let her find out for herself, but then it would be too late. Weren't parents supposed to try to help their kids navigate big life decisions?

"Colleen, you're a smart, beautiful, independent woman. I just want to make sure that you're making the right decision, and honestly, I don't think you are."

"Well, there it is. No second-guessing what you mean."

"I just want to say what I think and then you can make the decision, and I will support you no matter what. But, I don't think Peter is the one for you. I don't feel like he cares as much about your needs as you care about his. I don't know why he asked you to marry him."

"Wow, mom! What a terrible thing to say! Because he loves me?"

"Does he?"

"I can't believe you're being so mean about this! I think I want to go back to the hotel now."

"Colleen, please don't walk away. Just answer me this one thing."

Colleen stood there, her arms crossed, something she had done her whole life when she was upset. "Fine. What?"

"When you think about being married and becoming a mother and raising your children to be good people, do you see Peter standing there beside you, towing the line? Do you see him nurturing your kids? Do you see him coaching you when you're giving birth? Do you see him standing there next to you when you're having the worst day of your life? You don't have to answer me. But think about it. And if that is the man that you see standing beside you no matter what, for better or for worse, then you marry him. But if you have any doubts whatsoever, that is your gut and God telling you to make a different decision."

Colleen didn't say anything, and they started walking back toward her hotel. All Julie could do was hope that she had somehow gotten her daughter to at least think clearly about this major life decision she was making.

JANINE STARED at the computer screen. "I'm still not sure exactly how this is supposed to help me get more students."

"Having your own Facebook page is going to give people a place to go, especially since you don't have a website. That's another thing we need to add to our list," William said, writing it down.

"I just teach yoga! On the beach! I don't even have a location. How can I possibly need all of this technology?"

He chuckled. "Boy, you really have something against technology, don't you?"

"I think for the most part it's the bane of our existence. People always staring at their phones and sending texts. What happened to just good old-fashioned conversation?" Janine said, throwing up her hands. Dixie clapped from behind the counter.

"I agree! For instance, it would be really nice if my son would stop texting me and actually give his old mother a call every now and again!"

William rolled his eyes. "Mom, when I call you, I end up on the phone for over an hour learning about all the gossip from people in town that I don't even know. Mary Evans had hip replacement. George O'Donnell tried to kick a pigeon. Eleanor Crawford's niece got a scholarship to Duke..."

"That's called good conversation, son," she said as she passed him walking to the inventory room to get a new stack of books to display.

"Well, anyway, you need to have all of this lined up so that people can find you. Facebook is a great way to do that. We can even set up some ads if we need to."

"I'm pretty sure I don't need to be running ads until I'm making enough money."

"It's just something to add to our list," William said.

"*Our* list?"

"Well, I'm helping you so it's *our* list." He looked

down at the sheet of paper and wrote something on the long list of activities they were going to do to get more people to come to her classes. Janine had to stifle a smile as she thought about how rocky their relationship had started off, but how they had become fast friends who seemed to understand each other.

"I'm starving. Can we at least walk down to the sandwich shop ?"

"Fine," William said, folding the piece of paper and closing the laptop. "Let's go feed you. I wouldn't want you to get any weaker."

She smacked him on the shoulder. "I think I have shown you I'm not weak."

He smiled. "Yes, ma'am, you have definitely shown me that."

They waved goodbye to Dixie and walked out of the bookstore onto the street. Janine had a favorite sandwich shop that had a chicken salad sandwich to die for. As they walked, they chatted about this and that, including all of the dramatics around Colleen's engagement. William was careful not to give his opinion too much, although he would chime in here and there.

"So, how are you liking your new job?" she asked. She didn't know exactly when he worked because he always seemed to be around. They had continued their tradition of meeting on the beach every morning, even when it was freezing cold. They just dressed warmer and continued meditating and doing yoga. They would continue paddle boarding once the weather warmed up again.

"I like it. I'm getting to work from home a lot, which is nice. And helping you out is honing my marketing skills."

"Good. I'm glad that everything is going so well for you."

"There is one thing that is not going well."

"Really? What is that?"

"Well, there's this woman that I'm interested in. I want to ask her out, but I can't tell if she's interested in me."

"Interesting. What makes you think that she might not be interested?"

"She's a little abrasive at times, kind of sarcastic. But, then there are other times I find her quite endearing."

"She sounds like quite a catch," she said with a laugh.

"I think she is. But she's also quite a pain in the butt sometimes."

"Well, don't you want a woman who can give you a run for your money?" she asked, smiling.

"Maybe. So, how would you suggest that I ask a woman like this out?"

"I think you just have to ask. It sounds like she's a no nonsense kind of gal."

"Would you say something like, 'How would you

like to have dinner with me tonight?"

"I don't know. That seems kind of ambivalent. Like, I'm not sure she'll know that you're actually asking her out on a date rather than just a friendly meal. I think you have to make it more specific."

"Like what?"

"Like maybe ask her if she would like to go ice-skating and then to a very nice restaurant. I think that makes it seem like more of an intimate evening between two people who like each other rather than just a friendly night of eating."

"I see what you're saying. So, I should make it very much known that I think she's beautiful and really cool and I would like to see her on a more official basis?"

"Right. I think that's definitely the way to go."

"Got it."

They walked along quietly for a few moments, Janine trying not to break out in full-blown giggles.

"So, I was wondering, how do you feel about ice-skating, Janine?"

She laughed. "I have no idea. I've never been."

"Me either. How would you like to go try to teach each other tonight, say around seven o'clock? Then maybe we can grab a bite at a very nice restaurant afterwards?"

"What a great idea. I accept your invitation!"

William nodded. "Excellent."

They might just be the most awkward and completely perfect for each other couple in town.

"I DON'T KNOW why I'm so nervous about saying goodbye to Colleen. I feel like I handled things badly with her yesterday." Julie sat across the table from her sister, her head in her hands.

"I think you told her the truth, at least as you see it. And if it helps, I agree with you. I think that guy is all wrong for our Colleen."

"It's so hard. I don't want to be one of those meddling mothers, like ours. But at the same time, I'm terrified she's going to sign herself up for a life of misery. I just don't want her to give up on all of her dreams."

"Colleen has a good head on her shoulders. I think she'll make the right decision in the end. "

Just then, there was a knock at the door. She opened it, and Michael was standing there.

"Michael, what are you doing here?"

"Can I come in?"

"If you must," she said. Michael walked into the house and immediately met the death stare from Janine. So far, the two of them had not run into each other since he'd been in town, but now was the time.

Janine stood up and slowly walked across the

room to face him. "What on God's green earth are you doing here? Have you not done enough?"

"Janine, please."

"No, it's fine. Everybody else has said their piece to me. Why not her?" Michael said, crossing his arms. "Janine never liked me anyway."

"Well, that's because I could smell your deception from a mile away."

"I was a good husband for a long time!" Michael said, pointing his finger at her.

"You better put that finger down before I break it off," Janine said, stepping closer to him.

"You two, stop it! I'm stressed out enough without all of this going on!"

Janine stepped back. "I'm sorry, Julie. It's just I haven't gotten to say what I wanted to say for a long time."

"I just can't handle this right now," Julie said. She looked out the window to see if her daughter was driving up, but she wasn't. Colleen was supposed to have been there twenty minutes before. She was worried that maybe she wasn't even going to come say goodbye before she boarded her plane back to California.

"I just wanted to come by here and let you know that I'm sorry for everything I did to you, Julie. I know I said it before, but I really want you to understand how sorry I am. I ruined our marriage. I acted like a gigantic jerk. But I really want us to be able to get along for our daughters. "

"I agree, Michael. I don't even hold any ill will for you anymore. I hope that you and Victoria make a happy life, but you have to understand that everybody who saw me go through this really wants to strangle you."

"Amen," Janine said under her breath.

"Janine," Julie said, shooting her a look.

Janine held up her hand and mouthed the word sorry.

"I see that you have made a really nice life for yourself here, and I just want you to know that you deserve it. You were a very good wife to me, and even when I got hurt, I took advantage of you all over again. Maybe it's a midlife crisis or something. I don't know what made me do what I did, but I'm trying to make the best of it. And, if I'm being honest, I regret every bit of it. Victoria is not the woman you are. There were times I thought I might want to try to get you back, but then I realized I don't deserve you. And I have a son, so I'm trying to make it work with her."

"Michael, why are you telling me all of this?"

"I don't know. I guess I just needed to get it off my chest before we left. And don't worry, we're not going to move down here close to you. You know how I hate the beach."

"That I do."

"Well, I better go."

"Wait, you're not going to say goodbye to Colleen?"

"No. Our plane leaves in a couple of hours, so we've got to head out. She and I spoke on the phone this morning."

"Oh. Well, have a safe trip back to Boston."

Michael waved and walked out the door. Julie felt an immense sense of a weight being lifted off of her shoulders. He had apologized and he seemed to mean it. She in no way trusted him again, but that wasn't her problem. He wasn't her problem anymore. And she wished him well because everybody deserves happiness, even if they got it under false pretenses.

"Well, you're a better woman than I am," Janine said, putting her arm around Julie.

"There's nothing to be gained by hating him anymore. I feel sorry for him in a way. He's never going to know what true love is because I don't think he's capable of feeling it."

"Is that Colleen pulling up out there?"

Julie looked out the window and saw the cab pull up with her daughter inside.

When she opened the door, she saw something she didn't expect to see. Her daughter was standing there, suitcase in hand, puffy red eyes from crying.

"Oh, Colleen, what happened?"

"I left Peter."

"What?"

"I thought about what you said. I was just settling, and I don't want to do that."

Julie was so relieved, even though she knew her daughter was very hurt in that moment. "Colleen, I'm so sorry, but I know you made the right decision. A mother's heart just knows."

She pulled her daughter into a tight hug, rubbing her back like she did when she was a little girl.

Janine picked up her suitcase and brought her into the house. They all sat down on the sofa.

"I just couldn't quit thinking about those questions you asked me. So I started talking to him about what he wanted as far as family and career and where we would live. Everything was involving his family and not mine. It seemed like he wanted to keep me away from the people who love me, and I know that's the first sign of an abuser. I just couldn't do it. But now, my whole life is in upheaval."

"I know you were living together, but I'll help you get your things moved…"

"I'm not really worried about that right now. What I want to ask you though is do you mind if I stay here for a few months? I really want to think about what I want to do with my life. I wasn't happy with my position out in California, so maybe I could find something closer to here?"

Julie grinned from ear to ear. "Are you serious?

You want to live here and work close by? Of course, you can stay as long as you want!"

Colleen laughed, tears still streaming down her face at times. "You aren't a little excited are you?"

"Honey, the best thing I could ever ask for is to have my daughter home. I will help you figure out what to do with your life. I'll help you do whatever you need to. I'm just so glad to have you back!"

our weeks later

If there was one thing that Julie had learned, it was that a lot can change in just a few weeks. Having her daughter home with her for the last month had been such a blessing. They had gotten to catch up on so much lost time, and she couldn't imagine ever living so far away from her again.

There was just something about knowing a child once they were an adult. It was a different relationship than raising the same child. They were more like friends, although she still gave her motherly advice whether it was wanted or not.

Colleen had hit the ground running, much to Julie's surprise. She had found an assistant job at a local attorney's office that prosecuted a lot of domestic violence cases. She was thrilled to be involved in something that she believed in, so letting Peter go had proven to be easier than either one of them had anticipated.

Once her things were delivered, she set up her bedroom. Julie really enjoyed having both Janine and Colleen living in the house with her. They had a lot of girl time, going to get pedicures, shopping on the square and staying up late, drinking coffee and gossiping about anything and everything. It made Julie feel young again.

Things had also started to ramp up between her and Dawson. They had gone out on several dates, and Colleen greatly approved of him. They had forged their own relationship as friends, Dawson even going as far as taking Colleen on a kayak tour down the marsh. He wanted her to get to know the area so that she would stay and make Julie happy.

Janine and William had also been spending more time together, with him often dropping in on her yoga classes on the beach. The marketing had paid off greatly, and now she regularly had fifteen to twenty people in her morning classes. Things were going so well that she was already thinking about getting her own space near the square sometime before summer.

As Julie stood in the kitchen, snapping green beans and throwing them into a pot for Sunday dinner, she thought about all of the many blessings that just accumulated right in front of her.

She thought about how when hard times hit, it's so easy to think things will always be bad. But, somehow, instead of things getting worse, they got better. When her marriage fell apart, she worried that her life would never be the same again, and it wouldn't. But not in a bad way.

It wouldn't be the same because now she and her sister had a great relationship.

It wouldn't be the same because now she had a totally different kind of man in her life.

It wouldn't be the same because she had a spitfire for a new best friend and business partner.

It wouldn't be the same because her beautiful daughter was now living with her and becoming one of her best friends.

She put the beans on to boil and then turned her attention to peeling some potatoes.

"Anything I can help with?" Colleen asked as she walked into the kitchen.

"Actually, yes. If you can start making the sweet tea, that would be great."

"What time is everyone supposed to be here?"

"Sunday dinner starts at twelve o'clock, on the dot."

"Who all is coming this week?"

"Well, I know Janine invited William. Of course, Dawson is coming."

"Of course," Colleen said with a smile.

"And we also have Dixie coming this week. She's

going to give us an update on her treatment, but judging from what I've seen at work, she's doing really well."

"I'm so glad. I know I've only known her for a month, but I feel like she's my grandma!"

"Well I wouldn't tell your real grandmother that," Julie said with a laugh.

"Oh, never," Colleen said, smiling. "I heard from Dad today."

"Oh yeah? And what did he have to say?"

"He's starting some new kind of rehab. Also, they had Charlie's first birthday party. He sent me a few pictures."

"Good. I'm glad you are able to have a relationship with your father."

Julie had really worked on her negative feelings about Michael. Now, she was trying to focus on the good times they had as a family and not so much on the way things ended. Plus, she figured he was Victoria's problem now.

"What still needs to be done?" Janine asked as she walked into the kitchen.

"Can you check the roast in the oven?"

"Roast? Are you sure this one is going to eat it?" Janine asked, squeezing Colleen's shoulder.

"Don't worry. I'm in South Carolina now. I've decided to only be a part-time vegan."

Julie chuckled. "I'm not sure that's a thing."

The three women spent the next hour in the

kitchen together, preparing everything for Sunday dinner. They carried it all to the table, including a blueberry pie that Julie had made the night before. She was getting very accustomed to cooking a lot because it seemed like she always had company at her house.

Just before noon, Dawson and William walked into the house with Dixie trailing not far behind. They had picked her up on the way to the house so that she didn't have to drive her car. Dawson was still very overprotective, as well as William.

"Happy Sunday!" Dixie said. "I brought the rolls!"

"Yay ! I love your yeast rolls!" Julie said, taking the covered basket from her hands and giving her a quick kiss on the cheek.

Dawson met her in the kitchen and pulled her into a tight hug. "Good morning, beautiful," he said before planting a kiss on the top of her head. Things were getting more serious with them by the day, but Julie had no more qualms about it. She knew exactly the man he was.

"Good morning, yourself. Thanks for picking Dixie up."

He smiled. "Of course. We couldn't have Sunday dinner without our adoptive mother, could we?" She rose up on her tiptoes and kissed him on the cheek.

"No PDA in the kitchen!" William said as he walked in to put down a tray of cupcakes that Dixie had apparently brought also.

"PDA isn't so bad," Janine said as she walked up behind him and poked him in the side.

"Why on earth did Dixie bring cupcakes? We already have a pie. There aren't enough people here to eat this many calories!" Julie said with a laugh.

Everyone sat down at the table and joined hands to say grace. This was something that had become a tradition, and it reminded Julie of her days growing up with her parents. Grace was an important part of Sunday dinner, and really any meal around at their table.

"Dear Lord, we thank you for this food and for everyone sitting around this table. Please help the food to nourish our bodies and keep us all safe. Thank you for your many blessings. Amen." Dawson was usually the one who said the prayer, and he did a great job at it.

"Let's dig in!" Julie said. Everyone started talking and laughing and passing dishes of food around. She was happy to see Dixie in such a good mood. Her medication changes and the adjoining therapy seemed to have stalled at the progress of her disease, and she was back to her old self, cracking jokes and poking fun at everyone.

When they were in the middle of their meal, Julie heard someone knock at the door. For a moment, she looked around the table trying to figure out who could be out there. Everybody she knew and loved was sitting with her.

"Well, that can't be William and his sour face because he's sitting right there," Dawson said. William tossed part of a roll at him, nailing him on his arm.

"You're going to regret that," Dawson said with a chuckle.

"I'll get it," Julie said. "And don't eat all of those mashed potatoes before I get back!"

She opened the door and saw the last person she ever expected to see standing there.

"Meg? Oh my gosh! What are you doing here?"

Within seconds, Colleen and Janine had run to the door as well, all of them taking turns hugging Julie's youngest daughter.

"Hey, everybody!" Meg said, a big smile on her face. Meg had always been her happiest kid, full of enthusiasm for whatever was going on at the time. Her tiny stature did not hide her huge personality.

"I'm so happy you're here, honey, but how? What's going on?"

Meg smiled. "I was a little jealous seeing my sister with you on social media, so I wanted to join in the fun."

"Well, come inside! Join the fun!" Julie said, very uneasy about her daughter's sudden appearance at her front door. None of this made sense, but she was so happy to have both of her children together in the same room that she didn't want to poke at it too much.

Meg walked inside as everyone started introducing themselves. Julie could tell she was a little bit overwhelmed, trying to keep up with all of the names and faces.

"I don't understand, sweetie. Are you able to just leave your school just like that?"

"Oh, I took a leave of absence from the program. Maybe I'll go back next school year. I just needed... a break. It was a lot of stress being that far from home."

"What about Christian?"

Meg's face dropped a bit. "That didn't work out."

"Oh, I'm sorry, honey. Well, you are so welcome here. I'm sure Colleen won't mind sharing a room with you again."

Colleen smiled. "I guess so. She's small, so we should be fine."

The sisters laughed and hugged each other. Janine glanced at Julie. The two of them both had worried looks on their faces.

But if there was one thing Julie had learned, it was to let things unfold slowly before reacting. And right now, that was all she knew to do.

MEG STOOD next to the bed, wishing she could climb in and fall asleep already, but Colleen was still brushing her teeth and making too much noise. It was only ten at night, but she was exhausted from a very long day of traveling. Thankfully, Colleen had work early in the morning and needed to hit the sack too.

"Are you going to miss Paris and all of the baguettes?" Colleen asked when she walked back into the room.

"The cheese was the best part. I swear I gained five pounds over there."

Colleen looked at her. "Just five? Are you sure?"

Meg glared at her. "Not nice."

"You know I was just joking, sis! You're still a tiny thing, as always."

"I better hit the bathroom one more time before bed. Are you done in there?"

"Yep. I'm going to write in my journal until you come out."

"Okay."

Meg walked into the bathroom and shut the door. She sat down on the closed toilet and took in a deep breath. This was the most stressed out she'd been in a long time, and she had second guessed her decision to come home during every moment of the flight. But, she didn't know what else to do.

She stood up and brushed her long, dark hair. She had done this every night since elementary school. One hundred brush strokes, no more and no less.

She turned and looked at the full length mirror

on the back of the door and stared into it. Her face was puffy from all the extra tears she'd shed recently, and her cheeks looked chubbier. Maybe that was just from all her beloved cheese.

Then, she turned sideways and carefully inspected her whole body. Were her thighs getting bigger? Was that a double chin? She had never been a vain person. This was more about self protection. She needed some time to figure out her next move, and keeping her secret was critical.

She put her hands on her lower abdomen and looked down. "I promise I'll make the best decision for you," she whispered, a tear rolling down her cheek.

"You coming out?" Colleen called from the other side of the door.

Meg wiped away the tear. "Yeah, coming right now," she said, before opening the door and crawling into bed.

CHECK out other Rachel Hanna books on your favorite book retailer's website!

CPSIA information can be obtained
at www.ICGtesting.com
Printed in the USA
LVHW090313260721
693675LV00011B/301